Cry at Midnight

MAVIS GULLIVER

INDEPENDENT INNOVATIVE INTERNATIONAL

Published by Cinnamon Press,
Meirion House,
Tanygrisiau,
Blaenau Ffestiniog,
Gwynedd LL41 3SU
www.cinnamonpress.com

The right of Mavis Gulliver to be identified as author of this work
has been asserted by her in accordance with the Copyright, Designs
and Patent Act, 1988. © 2014 Mavis Gulliver.
ISBN 978-1-909077-35-5
British Library Cataloguing in Publication Data. A CIP record for
this book can be obtained from the British Library.
Designed and typeset in Palatino and Lucida by Cinnamon Press.
Cover design by Christopher Hull and Jacob Hull from original
artwork 'Moonlight Horse' by Destinyvispro © agency:
Dreamstime.com
Cinnamon Press is represented by Inpress and by the Welsh Books
Council in Wales.
Printed in Poland

Acknowledgements

I am grateful to Jan Fortune for having faith in my story, to the
team at Cinnamon Press for their unstinting support and to
Christopher Hull and Jacob Hull for designing the perfect cover.

Thanks to my husband Richard for my cabin on the shore and
for encouraging me to hide myself away to write; to tutors on
various courses for helping along the way - Joan Lennon,
Catherine MacPhail, Lorraine Mace and Linda Strachan; to my
grandchildren for getting involved in the story and for urging
me to finish the book. Last but not least, to the Isle of Tiree
where I saw the fencepost from which the story grew.

For my grandchildren
Josef, Cerys and Olive

Cry at Midnight

Chapter 1

It happened too quickly, one terrifying thing merging into another, the unearthly cry that invaded her sleep, the pounding of her heart, the hands that grabbed and shook her, and the scream that she couldn't hold back.

'Stop it, Merryn. Wake up.'

The shout, close to her ear, made her stop struggling. Gasping for breath, she stared at her brother's face glowing eerily in the torchlight.

'Get off me,' she said, 'I've got to find it.'

Before she could wriggle out of her sleeping bag, Hamish pinned her down. 'Don't be stupid. You haven't got to find anything. You've been dreaming. That's all.'

'It wasn't a dream.' She tried to push him away and her voice rose to a shout. 'Let me go.'

'No.' Hamish grasped her even more firmly.

'Then come with me,' she pleaded. 'Please.'

Hamish shook his head. 'I'm not going anywhere.'

'If Dad was here,' Merryn muttered, 'he'd help me. I know he would.'

'Well he isn't,' said Hamish, 'and it's no use asking Aunt Aggie. She won't help with anything. I thought she'd be pleased to see us, but she just looked down her big nose and sniffed as if we had something nasty on our shoes.'

Still holding Merryn down, he launched into an imitation of their great-aunt's words. 'You're only here as a favour to your dad and don't you forget it. Clean, tidy and quiet, that's what I expect. Break the rules and you'll be sorry. And don't call me Great Aunt Aggie. It makes me feel old, Aunt Aggie will do.'

He groaned and relaxed his grip. 'Fine holiday this is going to be. As for sleeping in a tent, the ground's as hard as a rock and my feet are freezing. I don't see why we can't sleep in the cottage.'

Merryn was barely listening. 'I don't care where I sleep,' she said. 'I just want to know what made the noise.'

'There wasn't a noise,' said Hamish.

'There was.' Her words tumbled out in a panic-stricken stream. 'And it wasn't a dream. I could hear it when I woke up. It was going on and on as if it couldn't stop. Then when it did stop, I could still hear it.'

She caught her breath, aware that she wasn't making sense. 'I mean it sort of stopped, but it's still inside my head.' She pushed her fingers in her ears and wiggled them frantically. Her head filled with a noise like thunder, but when she let her hands fall, the sound was still there.

'What am I going to do?' she wailed. 'What if it never goes away?'

Hamish stared at her. 'Of course it'll go away,' he said. 'You just have to wake up properly.'

'But I am awake,' Merryn insisted, 'and it wasn't a dream.' She shook her head in bewilderment. 'It was begging me to save it.'

Hamish gave a half-hearted laugh. 'That's crazy. People in dreams don't call for help.'

'It wasn't a person,' she said. 'It was an animal.'

'Well, that's even crazier,' said Hamish. 'Animals can't talk.'

'Hush! I'm thinking.' Merryn tried to catch the fragments of what had started as a dream. The fleeting glimpses were tantalising. But all she could remember was the frantic cry and the sense that something evil was swirling about in the darkness.

She clenched her fists in frustration. 'Of course it wasn't talking. It was… I know what it was. It was a horse. It was neighing, but it was a strange, frightened neigh and it woke me up. And when I was awake it carried on. That's how I know it wasn't a dream.'

'But why were you screaming?' Hamish asked. 'You're not scared of horses.'

Merryn's impatience grew. 'I wasn't frightened of the horse,' she snapped. 'I was frightened for it. Someone was hurting it and then you grabbed me. I didn't know it was you. That's why I screamed. There's a horse in trouble and I've got to go and save it.'

'Impossible, absolutely impossible,' said Hamish. 'You can't go out now.' He looked at his watch. 'It's ten past midnight and we've only been here a few hours. You wouldn't know where to look. You'd end up tumbling off a cliff, or falling into the sea and drowning. And it would be for nothing because there isn't a horse. It was nothing but a nightmare.'

He hooted with laughter and punched her on the shoulder. 'It was a nightmare, a mare calling in the middle of the night? Get it?'

Merryn scowled. 'Of course I get it, but it isn't funny.'

'Funny or not, I've had enough.' Hamish got back into his sleeping bag. 'And if you think I'm wasting my holiday searching for something out of a dream, you can think again.'

Merryn sighed. Hamish was right. Going out on her own would be foolish, but tomorrow she'd prove she was right. 'Just you wait,' she began.

'I'm not waiting for anything,' said Hamish as he switched off his torch.

The night closed around Merryn like a thick, black blanket. She'd never seen complete darkness before, and the shock of it made her burrow deep into her sleeping bag. Whatever had frightened the horse was out there and she couldn't see it. Even if it crept into the tent and sank its teeth into her she wouldn't know what it was. At this very moment it could be walking up the shingle path, creeping across the grass, tearing the tent flap. She stuffed her knuckles in her mouth and choked back a sob. She lay shivering with fright, too scared to sleep, too scared to run across the grass to the cottage. But eventually she must have slept, for when she opened her eyes a faint glow was filtering through the canvas. The black night was over.

The island was quiet, but the memory of the horse's cry was still inside her head. She peered at Hamish. He was snuffling in his sleep, so deep inside his sleeping bag that only a tuft of hair was sticking out. Careful not to wake him, she dressed and stepped out into the dawn light.

She'd been looking forward to running along the beach, but that would have to wait. Finding the horse was the only thing that mattered. She expected to find it in the field next to the cottage, but the only animals she could see were sheep. She jogged along the road to a farm, but there was no horse to be seen. She ran towards the sea, but there was no sign of a horse in the fields that bordered the track. She flopped down on the dune edge and put her head in her hands.

'It wasn't a dream,' she said. 'There's a horse somewhere and I've got to find it.'

Hoping to persuade Hamish to join in the search, she ran back to the tent. He wasn't there. Panic gripped her. The thing that frightened the horse! What if it had done something dreadful to him?

'Hamish,' she called as she stumbled towards the cottage. 'Hamish, are you there?'

As she pushed open the door, Aunt Aggie blocked her way. Scowling, her arms crossed in front of her bony body, she stared at Merryn with eyes as hard as stones.

'Well,' she demanded. 'What have you to say for yourself?'

Merryn flinched. 'N...nothing,' she whispered. 'I only went to look for the horse.'

'Horse! Don't talk nonsense. There aren't any horses hereabouts, and you've no business going out without telling me. What if you had an accident? You could be lost for days before anyone found you. You don't leave the garden again until I say you can.'

'But,' Merryn protested, 'I go out on my own at home.'

'Well, you're not at home now, and as long as you're on Tiree I'm in charge.' She turned and wagged a finger at Hamish.

He backed away and stuttered, 'I...I didn't do anything.

'I never said you did,' she snapped. 'Just let this be a warning. I won't tolerate bad behaviour. You've only been here one night and you've caused no end of worry. Now sit down and eat your porridge, both of you.'

Merryn took a tentative mouthful. It wasn't like the porridge they had at home. The saltiness was almost more than she could bear. She longed for a spoonful of brown sugar or a dribble of golden syrup.

Hamish dipped his spoon into his bowl and licked the end of it. 'Yuck!' he said. 'I can't eat this. It's...'

'It's all you're getting,' snapped Aunt Aggie.

'But I wanted...' He stopped as Merryn caught his ankle with the toe of her trainers.

Aunt Aggie thumped the table so hard that the spoons rattled in their saucers. 'There'll be no 'buts',' she said. 'I'm eighty four years old. I'm set in my ways. You eat what I eat or you go hungry. Is that clear?'

Hamish shuddered. He poked the porridge with his spoon, but he didn't eat a single mouthful. Merryn, after so much exercise was hungry. She forced herself to eat, but it was like taking medicine and she gagged every time she swallowed.

'You'll be sorry,' said Aunt Aggie to Hamish. 'Breakfast at seven is always porridge so you'd better get used to it. Meals are at twelve thirty and six. I expect you to be punctual and I don't want you bothering me in between.'

Merryn gasped. Staying with Aunt Aggie was going to be horrible. Why had mum and dad got business to attend to? Why had the Summer Camp been cancelled at the last minute? Why wasn't there another relation to stay with?

The change of plan hadn't bothered her at first because their great-gran, before she died, had told them wonderful stories about Tiree. Tears filled her eyes as she thought of the old lady with her cuddly body, gentle voice and curls that bounced when she laughed. Aunt Aggie's hair, scraped back in a bun made her ears stick out like jug handles. She was tall and skinny with a nose like a beak and a voice like an angry seagull. It was hard to believe that two such different people could be sisters.

Chapter 2

Hamish wiped his nose on the back of his hand. Merryn could see that he was close to tears. She had to do something to make him feel better. He wasn't a bad boy and there was no need for Aunt Aggie to be so strict.

'I'm sorry,' she began, 'it's just that everything here is different.' She swung her leg again and caught Hamish on the shin. 'Tell Aunt Aggie you'll do as you're told.'

Hamish didn't reply. He pushed his chair away from the table and ran out of the room. Aunt Aggie got to her feet, ready to follow, but Merryn was already at the door. She turned and forced a smile.

'I'm sorry. He's never been away from mum before and he's missing her. I'm sure he'll behave once he gets used to you.'

Aunt Aggie's face remained stern. She glared at Merryn. 'Well,' she said. 'You'd better be right, but after your escapade this morning I can't trust you either. You'd both be away on the next plane if I had somewhere to send you.'

No-one, not even the strictest teacher at school had ever spoken to Merryn like this. She bristled with indignation, but she took a deep breath and tried to explain.

'I'm sorry if I've done something wrong and I'm sorry if Hamish has upset you, but please give us a chance to put things right. Can I...' She stopped, gave a huge sigh and chewed on the side of her bottom lip. 'Can I...'

Aunt Aggie snapped. 'For goodness sake, girl, if you've something to say, spit it out.'

Merryn steadied herself with another deep breath. 'It's just that, well, the tent is all right for sleeping but there isn't room to do anything else. We're cramped...'

'Cramped!' Aunt Aggie snorted. 'You don't know the meaning of the word. When I was a girl there were eleven of us in this cottage, mother and father downstairs, five girls in one room upstairs and four boys in the other.'

'But Great Gran said that having so many brothers and sisters was fun,' said Merryn.

'She would say that.' Aunt Aggie's snort was even louder. 'She was everyone's favourite while I got blamed for everything. A room to yourself indeed! That's a luxury I would have liked, but I can't see why you need one.'

'I like to be quiet,' said Merryn. 'So does Hamish. We like to read without disturbing one another.'

'Fuss about nothing,' said Aunt Aggie. 'Reading! I don't have time for reading. And I can't be doing with you running up and down stairs like a pair of elephants.'

'We won't,' Merryn promised. 'We'll leave our shoes in the porch and go up and down on tiptoe. Besides, it's not just reading. We have homework. I have to find out about my ancestors, and Hamish has to keep a diary of his holiday. It's hard to do neat writing when you're sitting on the ground in a tent.'

Aunt Aggie seemed to consider for a moment, then she shook her head. 'No. You'll be up to mischief, bouncing on beds, breaking things, leaving grubby fingerprints everywhere.'

'We won't,' Merryn protested. 'We'll be quiet and careful, honestly we will. We'll be much less trouble if we have our own rooms. We fall out when we have to share. Please.'

Aunt Aggie muttered under her breath. 'Two days,' she said at last, 'you can have a two day trial. You still sleep in the tent though. I go to bed early and I'm not used to people in the house at night. Mind you, if you don't behave, you'll be back in the tent for the rest of your stay. Now get out from under my feet. I've things to do. You can choose a room and Hamish can have the other one, but mind you keep them tidy. It's not often I go upstairs these days, so you'd better take a duster with you.'

'Thank you.' In her eagerness, Merryn dashed through the door and put her foot on the first step before she remembered to take off her shoes. Then she tiptoed up the steep stairs, paused on the landing and opened the first door. The room looked as if it hadn't been used for a very long time, but at least there was a bed, a chest of drawers, a chair and a small table. She pulled the curtain aside, looked out of the window and wrinkled her nose in disappointment. There wasn't a sea view.

The other room was similar, but when she looked more closely, there was a difference. The wall behind the wardrobe was completely covered by a curtain. Maybe there was a sea view after all. She crossed the room, squeezed past the wardrobe and ducked behind the curtain. There was no sign of a window – just a dimly lit space filled with a rail of old clothes. Disappointed, she was turning away when a chink of light caught her eye. She pushed the coats aside and there, behind them, was a door. She tried the handle but the door wouldn't open. It was locked and there was no sign of a key.

A tingle of excitement ran from the top of her head to the tips of her toes. Strange things were happening, a horse where no horse should be, something scary in the island darkness, and a locked door. Perhaps the time on Tiree wouldn't be so dreadful after all.

'Hamish,' she called as she ducked into the tent. 'We still have to sleep in here but we can go upstairs during the day. Only listen, we're on trial for two days so you've got to behave. If we annoy Aunt Aggie she won't give us a second chance. Grab your things and I'll show you.'

Looking more cheerful, Hamish loaded his bag and followed. He took a quick look round and dumped his bag on the bed. 'So, what's your room like?'

'A bit smaller than yours,' she said.

'You won't mind me looking then.'

As Hamish pushed past her, Merryn followed. She crossed her fingers, hoping that he wouldn't notice the curtain.

'Same rules as at home,' he called over his shoulder as he left. 'No coming into one another's rooms without permission, and I'm going to make a notice so Aunt Aggie can't come in either.'

'Waste of time,' said Merryn, 'she's bound to ignore it.'

When Hamish had gone she started to search for the key. She went through the drawers and the wardrobe, but there was no key to be found. Jars on the windowsill didn't look promising either. One contained nothing but dust, a dead leaf and the

17

shrivelled remains of a spider. The other was full of dusty pebbles. She picked it up and turned it upside down. The pebbles tumbled onto the bed and there among them was a key. Breathless with anticipation she returned to the locked door and pushed the key into the lock. It fitted but was too stiff to turn. She grasped it with both hands and tried to force it, but it wouldn't move. Almost weeping with frustration she wiggled it about – up and down, in and out, from side to side, until, with a sudden click, it turned. She pushed the door open and stared wide-eyed into a small room with a tiny cobweb-covered window.

'It's a cubbyhole,' she whispered, 'my very own secret cubbyhole.'

As she shut the door behind her, a slight breeze lifted a cloud of dust. It filled her nose and she broke the silence with a string of coughs and sneezes. Gasping for breath, she pushed the window open, gulped the fresh air and looked down. Below her was the flat roof of the porch, the garden, fields, dunes and the sea. Satisfied that she had a sea view after all, she turned and looked round. A small desk stood against one wall and a pile of boxes lay in one corner; but more interesting by far was an old wooden chest. Absentmindedly, she began to doodle in the layer of dust on its surface. She drew a horse's head, framed it in a circle and wrote her name underneath. Merryn MacQueen.

'Merryn.'

Startled, she stopped and looked round. Had someone really spoken her name? She checked the bedroom and the landing. Both were empty. Sure that she'd been mistaken, she went back into the cubbyhole and wiped the writing away with her sleeve.

'Merryn MacQueen.'

She leapt back, her heart thumping so loudly that it seemed to fill the space around her. She chewed on her fingers and stared at the chest, her tummy churning with a mixture of fear and excitement. Had that dry dusty sound really come out of the chest? Cautiously she edged closer, then, with a sudden dash, she threw up the lid and jumped back. Nothing stirred. She craned her neck and peered inside, waiting for something to move, listening for the voice to speak.

Feeling foolish, she whispered, 'Is anyone there?'

All was quiet. All was still. Warily she reached out, snatched a book from the chest and stepped back. No voice came to disturb the silence.

She laughed nervously. 'Of course there isn't anyone there,' she said. 'How could there be?'

Convinced that she'd imagined the voice, she lifted out book after musty old book. Was there nothing else? Her disappointment grew, until, almost at the bottom, she found a bundle. It was wrapped in newspaper and tightly tied with string. Her jaw dropped in surprise, for the date on the newspaper told her that the bundle hadn't been opened for more than a hundred years.

At that moment she heard Aunt Aggie's voice. Hastily she slipped out of the cubbyhole, straightened the curtain and opened her bedroom door.

'Come down at once,' Aunt Aggie shouted. 'You can go for a walk before the weather changes. There'll be heavy showers this afternoon.'

Aching with disappointment, Merryn locked the door and returned the key to the jar. The contents of the parcel would have to wait.

Chapter 3

'Out you go,' said Aunt Aggie. 'Get rid of all that surplus energy then you might behave yourselves. Go down the track and along the beach but don't go past the headland. I need to know exactly where you are.'

Hamish was outside almost before Aunt Aggie had finished speaking.

Merryn on the other hand was filled with frustration. 'I'd rather finish what I was doing,' she said.

'There's time enough for that.' Aunt Aggie was adamant. 'Go out and don't come back until lunch time.'

'Why is she so horrible?' Hamish asked as they jogged down the track. 'She's a miserable old cow. I bet she never smiled in her entire life.'

'Maybe she has reasons,' said Merryn. 'Maybe she's full of aches and pains, or maybe she's just not used to children.'

'Well, whatever it is,' said Hamish, 'she's not going to spoil my first run on the beach.'
Whooping excitedly, he ran towards the sea, scattering gulls that were preening along the shore. Merryn wandered along the tide line, her mind turning on the parcel that had been hidden long ago.

'Hurry up, Merryn. Last one to the headland's a rotten egg.' Hamish set off, his feet pounding the damp sand, his elbows pumping.

Merryn knew she couldn't beat him so she didn't even try. By the time she joined him he was on his knees, peering into a rock pool, the race forgotten.

'I need a book. I know that's a crab, but I don't know what this is.' He pointed to a dark red blob. 'I want to find out about everything for my holiday diary.'

Merryn, anxious to get back to the parcel, sat on a rock and watched the waves until it was time to head back for lunch. They ran all the way, but by the time they reached the cottage it was twelve thirty four and their food was already on the table.

'Serve you right if it's cold,' said Aunt Aggie. 'Twelve thirty I said, and twelve thirty I meant.'

'Thank you for my lunch,' said Hamish when the silent meal was over. 'It was very nice and I'm sorry we were late.'

Merryn looked at him in surprise. It was obvious that he was about to ask for something. She tried to hide a smile when he cleared his throat and took a big breath.

'I...I don't suppose you have a book about sea creatures,' he said. 'I need one for my homework,'

'Indeed I don't.' said Aunt Aggie, 'and it beats me why anyone would want one. But if it'll keep you out of mischief I'll see if Donald can help.'

She picked up the phone and began to speak in Gaelic. Merryn listened, but although Great Gran had taught her a few Gaelic songs, she had no idea what the conversation was about.

Aunt Aggie put the phone down and explained. 'Donald lives in the cottage next door. You can go and see him at three o'clock. He's lived here all his life and has lots of books. He'll be able to tell you what you want to know.'

'Why can't I go now?' Hamish grumbled.

Aunt Aggie glared. 'Because it isn't three o'clock,' she said. 'Now get out from under my feet. Go on, find something to do.'

Hamish went to his room to start his book and Merryn went back to the cubbyhole. Heart thumping, she put the parcel on the desk and started to pick at the knots with her fingernails. When the last one was untied the newspaper fell open. Carefully, hardly daring to breathe, she unfolded the woollen shawl that lay inside. As the fabric slipped back her mouth opened in a huge and silent O.

Her first finger began to tingle. It took on a life of its own. It reached out to stroke the wooden box that had been hidden more than a hundred years ago. It touched the intricate carving and began to follow the curves of the pattern. Round and round it went until she thought she'd reached the beginning. But there was no beginning, and there was no end. The pattern went on and on in a way that breathed of mysteries.

Her imagination took flight. There was treasure inside, a secret that had been lost for years. Eagerly she lifted the lid. The box was empty. There was no treasure. But there was no time for disappointment, for on the inside of the lid, carved in beautiful letters was her name - *MERRYN MACQUEEN*.

'Merryn MacQueen. You have come at last. Wear the necklace and all will be revealed.'

Her hands flew to her mouth. How could a voice come out of an empty box? It was impossible. It was too scary for words. She reached out to close the lid, but as soon as her fingers touched it, the voice came again.

'Merryn MacQueen, do you want to save the horse?'

'Yes! Yes of course I do, only I...' Her words tailed away and she shrank back shuddering with apprehension.

'Do not be afraid,' said the voice. 'I think you are the one we have been waiting for. If I am right, you are the only one who can save the horse. Do as I ask. Wear the necklace and all will be revealed.'

Questions filled her head, questions so strange that they may never be answered. Why is my name on the box? How can they, whoever they are, have been waiting for me? How do they even know about me? Can I really save the horse? Why does it need saving? Dare I wear the necklace?

That was the one question she could answer. If it really would help to save the horse, she would try. But the box was empty and she had no idea where the necklace was hidden.

'You must find the necklace for yourself,' said the voice. 'Only then will we know that you are the one we have been waiting for.'

She turned the box over and over in her hands. There was a soft sliding noise as if something was moving inside. She tipped it upside down and looked for a hidden compartment. The base was the only possible place, but how could she get into it? She rapped it with her knuckles, she pressed it and pushed it, but it wouldn't move.

She searched for a knob, a button or a lever, but there was nothing. The only things that stood out were two metal handles, each shaped like a figure of eight. She turned them together, away from her, then towards her. She turned them in opposite directions, but still nothing happened. Suddenly, the answer came. She turned the box upside down and turned them again. There was a click, the base of the box lifted, and there inside was a linen bag.

'It's the necklace. It must be,' she whispered as her hand slipped inside.

Would it be made of gold? Would it be strung with jewels? As she pulled it out, her shoulders dropped with disappointment. There was no gold. There were no jewels. It was the strangest necklace she'd ever seen. It wasn't even made of beads. There were just stones and smooth brown things strung together on a knotted thread.

Now that she'd seen it, her determination wavered. How could such a strange necklace help to save the horse? She dropped it back in the box, turned away and stared out of the window. It was all too strange for words. What should she do? What could she do?

'Merryn,' the voice came again. 'You found the necklace. You are the one we have been waiting for. Wear it now and all will be revealed.'

Against her will, she was drawn back to the box. Tentatively, she picked up the necklace and ran it through her fingers. She couldn't find a beginning or an end. There wasn't a join anywhere. She held it above her head and tried to find the courage to wear it. As it caught on her hair, the horse's cry sounded so clearly that she winced at the strength of it. It was a momentary thing, a sudden urgent call that ended almost before it had begun. There was a horse, and the necklace would help her to find it. Holding her breath she let the necklace go. It slipped over her head and dropped onto her shoulders. Immediately, the room grew brighter and the whole world seemed suddenly larger.

'Tell me what to do,' she whispered. 'I can feel the magic, but I don't know how to use it'

There was no reply. Were there no instructions? She looked inside the bag, and there, tucked in the corner was a square of paper. She unfolded it carefully and scanned the lines of faint spidery writing. It must be Gaelic, for there wasn't a single word she could understand. Or was there? Suddenly, one word stood out from all the rest, a word that sent a thrill right through her body. In her eagerness, she forgot Aunt Aggie's bad temper.

'I found something,' she called as she ran downstairs. 'I found a note, but the only word I can read is Merryn. Is it Gaelic? What else does it say?'

Aunt Aggie turned angrily. 'I said you could use the room. I didn't say you could poke around in things that don't concern you. And can't you see I'm resting?' She put on her glasses, snatched the scrap of paper from Merryn and looked at it closely.

'It's Gaelic right enough,' she said. 'I'm not very good at reading it, but it does say Merryn. Perhaps it has something to do with my great-grandmother. Maybe she wrote it. She was...'

'Tell me later,' Merryn interrupted. 'Read the note first, please.'

Aunt Aggie frowned as she ran her finger under the lines. Merryn couldn't keep still. She clasped and unclasped her hands. She was desperate to know the meaning of every single word.

Aunt Aggie's frown grew deeper and deeper, and when she'd finished reading, she shook her head.

Merryn couldn't hide her impatience. 'Well, what does it say?'

'A lot of nonsense,' said Aunt Aggie, 'and I refuse to fill your head with it.' She turned away, screwed the note into a ball and tossed it towards the fire.

Chapter 4

'No!' Merryn screamed as she dashed to snatch the paper from the hearth. Breathing heavily she turned on Aunt Aggie and stamped her foot. 'It's mine,' she shouted. 'It's got my name on it. You've no right to burn it.'

Aunt Aggie's reply came through clenched teeth. 'Don't you dare speak to me like that, and it isn't yours. This house is mine and so is everything in it.'

Biting back the angry words that filled her head, Merryn put the paper on the table and smoothed out the creases. It would tell her how to save the horse, she was sure of it. She had to know what it said. Tears coursed down her cheeks. She sniffed and wiped them away with the back of her hand.

'You've got to tell me,' she sobbed. 'You're not being fair.'

Aunt Aggie passed a weary hand over her forehead. 'I don't have to tell you anything, but I'll tell you this. It's full of superstitions. It belongs to the past and that's where it's going to stay. Forget it.'

'I can't,' Merryn said, 'and I won't. I need it for my project. It's my family history and I have a right to know. If you won't tell me I'll work it out for myself.'

She grabbed the Gaelic Dictionary, one of only two books that lay on the dresser. She ran up to her bedroom, angry with Aunt Aggie for being so unhelpful, and angry with herself for losing her temper. Still shaking from her outburst she threw herself on the bed and looked at the words through a blur of tears. She tried to find them in the dictionary, but she couldn't make out the meaning at all. After a while she heard footsteps on the stairs.

Aunt Aggie was on her way. Not knowing what else to do, she pushed the letter under the bed and turned to face the door. Aunt Aggie burst in with a frown on her face.

'Let's get one thing clear,' she said. 'Don't ever speak to me in that disrespectful way again. But I'll tell you this. The note is about magic, the sort of magic they believed in long ago. It goes against common sense and I'll hear no more about it. Now do you understand?'

'No, I don't. Please, tell me,' Merryn begged. 'I won't believe it if it's nonsense. I just need it for my homework. Please tell me what it says.'

Aunt Aggie shook her head and sat down on the bed. It was as if all the anger had tired her out. Merryn almost felt sorry for her, but the feeling quickly passed. She simply had to know what was in the note. Nothing else mattered.

'Please,' she coaxed. 'Please.'

There was a long pause. Merryn held her breath and waited anxiously.

'I'm not happy about telling you,' said Aunt Aggie, 'but I suppose it is part of your history. And if it's for school I haven't really got a choice. Mind you, you must think of it as a story because that's all it is. There's not a grain of truth in it and that's a fact. It's about a necklace that can only be seen by people who have The Gift. It's ridiculous. A thing is either there or it isn't. And if it's there it stands to reason that everyone can see it.'

A shiver ran down Merryn's spine. She was wearing the necklace. It was round her neck. It was as plain as the nose on her face and Aunt Aggie hadn't seen it. She could hardly breathe for the excitement building up inside her. Exactly what 'The Gift' was, she had no idea. All she knew was that Aunt Aggie hadn't got it, and she had. It was true. That's why she'd heard the horse. That's why the voice from the box had spoken to her. That's why she could see the necklace. She looked up expecting more, but Aunt Aggie's lips were firmly closed.

'You can't stop now.' Merryn said. 'There must be more. There's got to be more.'

'Well if there is, I'm not telling you,' said Aunt Aggie. 'It's nonsense. An invisible necklace indeed! All I can say is I'm glad it's invisible. Otherwise you'd be searching for that as well as the horse.'

Merryn felt like screaming but she knew it would do no good. She forced herself to speak calmly. 'I want to know the rest because it has to go in my project,' she insisted. 'The teacher told us to find out as much as we could. So why won't you tell me?'

Aunt Aggie turned to leave. Then she stopped and seemed to reconsider. 'I won't say another word about the necklace but I'll tell you about my great-grandmother and you can put that in your project. She was called Merryn too. I don't know much because she was very old when I was just a wee girl. I think she lived to be a hundred and three. Her eyes were brown with golden flecks. I always felt that she could see right through me. Some people said she dealt in magic and that frightened me so I kept out of her way.'

She paused and looked at Merryn properly for the first time. 'Come to think of it, your eyes are the same. Strange that, it seems they missed a generation or two.'

Merryn's excitement grew and grew. She did a quick calculation on her fingers. 'Wow!' she said. 'So my great-great-great-great-grandmother had the same name and the same colour eyes as me. That's awesome. Please tell me more.'

'When I was a girl, she lived next door; but this cottage was her home for most of her life. She made medicines from plants. A few people thought she was a witch but others thought she had The Gift.'

The Gift! There was the word again. It echoed round Merryn's head and set her heart thumping.

'What is it?' she asked. 'What is The Gift?'

'It's nonsense,' said Aunt Aggie. She sniffed disapprovingly. 'Some people call it the sixth sense. Normal people have five senses and a few crazy people think they have an extra one. They claim to see things that aren't there. I think they have too much imagination, and that's all I'm going to say.'

'But the letter, tell me what's in it,' Merryn pleaded.

'I said no and I meant no and I'll not hear another word about it.' Aunt Aggie seemed to regain her strength. She held out her hand. 'Give it to me now. And this time I'll make sure it lands in the fire.'

'No!' Merryn shook her head and backed away. 'I won't. It has my name on it. It's mine. I won't give it to you. Not ever!'

Aunt Aggie stepped towards her. She raised her hand, and for an awful moment Merryn expected the sting of a slap across her face. But Aunt Aggie faltered.

She dropped her hand. Her face paled and she looked at Merryn through narrowed eyes.

'I'll get it,' she said, 'whether you give it to me or not. I will not knowingly have such unholy things under my roof. And don't think you'll get the better of me, because you won't.'

When Aunt Aggie had gone, Merryn was still shaking with anger. She waited until her heart had stopped thumping before picking up the letter and tucking it in the pocket of her jeans. Whatever happened, whatever Aunt Aggie said or did, she was determined to save the horse. The letter had to be translated and if it told her to make magic that's what she'd do. She wouldn't be able to stop herself. She had The Gift, but it would have to be a secret. She couldn't tell anyone because no-one would believe her. She could hardly believe it herself.

Just before three o'clock Hamish knocked on her door.

'Come on,' he said, 'we can go and see Donald now.'

Glad to leave the cottage, Merryn followed him downstairs. Aunt Aggie, standing tight-lipped by the gate didn't say a word, but Merryn could sense her anger. She was afraid that when they came back, they would no longer be allowed to use the bedrooms. But for now it would be good to have someone else to talk to. She crossed her fingers and hoped that Donald would be friendlier than Aunt Aggie.

The old man must have been waiting for them because he opened the door before they had time to knock. Unlike Aunt Aggie he smiled broadly and gave them each a hearty handshake.

'Come in and welcome,' he said. 'I'm pleased to see youngsters interested in the island and the wildlife. Now which one of you wants to know about rock pools?'

'Me,' said Hamish. 'I found crabs and things that look like blobs of jelly and I don't know what they are.'

'They'll be sea anemones,' said Donald, 'but if you go pottering about the shore you'll be finding lots of other creatures too.'

He led them to the table where books were waiting. 'Now these are special,' he said. 'You can come and look at them from time to time, but this one's a field guide. You can take it with you when you go to the shore. Just try not to get it wet.'

Hamish could hardly contain his delight. 'Thanks. Can I go now?' he asked.

'Wait a minute,' said Donald as he opened a small rucksack. 'You can take this too. There are collecting boxes, a magnifying glass, binoculars and other things you might find useful. You can use them as long as you look after them carefully.'

'Wow! This is brilliant. It's better than Christmas.' Hamish rummaged through the rucksack, put it on his back, called his thanks and disappeared through the door.

Donald chuckled. 'Such enthusiasm,' he said. 'I wish I could go with him but my old legs aren't up to it. Now, young lady, tell me, is there anything I can do for you?'

Chapter 5

Merryn checked that Hamish was out of earshot. She gave Donald an excited smile and lowered her voice to a whisper. 'There is. Only it's a secret.'

She lifted the scrap of paper out of her pocket and placed it in front of Donald. 'I found this and I want to know what it says.'

'Goodness me!' he exclaimed. 'This was written by Merryn MacQueen. I can hardly believe it. Do you know she lived in this very cottage?'

Merryn nodded. 'Yes, did you know her?'

'Bless me, no,' he said, 'she died before I was born. I wish I had though. I heard tell she was a fine woman, a great healer and a wonderful storyteller. She was clever too, one of the few who could read and write the Gaelic. Didn't Aggie tell you about her?'

'Only a bit,' said Merryn. 'She said she was scared of her. She thought she was a witch.'

'Never,' said Donald. 'She was a wise woman, that's all. But surely, Aggie read the note to you?'

Merryn shook her head. 'She said it was about an invisible necklace. Then she said it was superstitious nonsense and I wasn't to get mixed up in it. She said she was no good at reading Gaelic, but I didn't believe her. I think she lied because she didn't want me to know. She even tried to burn it only I managed to stop her. She got really angry and said she'd get hold of it and burn it anyway. I'm afraid I got angry too. We had a real row.'

Donald laughed. 'Good girl,' he said, 'only don't tell her I said so. Aggie is a very determined woman, but between you and me she isn't always right. So I don't blame you for standing up to her.'

He turned back to the note. 'Now let me translate it for you. Then we'll make a copy just in case Aggie gets her hands on it. You must take care of it though. It's part of your history and it would be a tragedy if it ended up in the fire.'

Like Aunt Aggie, he ran his finger under the lines, but unlike her, he nodded enthusiastically. Merryn sat on the edge of her seat, gripping the chair arms, trying to control her impatience.

'Aggie was right. It's about an invisible necklace but it's not as simple as that. It's only invisible to ordinary mortals. On the other hand, those humans who have The Gift can see it. If they wear it, they can connect with magical beings. The strange thing is that there isn't a description. There's nothing to say what it's made of, who made it or where it came from. I'd give anything to know.'

'You believe it,' Merryn exclaimed. 'You do, don't you?'

He laughed. 'Well, let's say I don't disbelieve it. We mortals don't know everything, and Merryn MacQueen had an uncanny way of knowing more than most.'

'I can...' She stopped as something warned her not to tell him that she had The Gift. 'I can copy the words into my diary,' she said, 'and if you make a copy too the words will be safe for ever. But doesn't it say anything else? Doesn't it say what it can be used for?'

Donald scanned the letter again. 'No, apparently the person who finds it has to discover that for themselves.'

Merryn's heart sank. Donald had translated the note but it didn't tell her how to rescue the horse. The voice would have to help her. But what if Aunt Aggie stopped her from using the bedroom? If she couldn't get into the cubbyhole she wouldn't be able to ask. There was no time to waste. She thanked Donald and ran back to the cottage. Her only chance was to sneak into her room without Aunt Aggie noticing.

But Aunt Aggie did notice. She was standing at the bottom of the stairs waiting to usher Merryn into the kitchen.

'I have things I want to say,' she said, 'but I'm so upset I don't know where to start. While I'm thinking about it you can help me with the housework.'

Merryn was desperate to get into the cubbyhole, but she knew she would have to do as she was told. Almost choking with frustration she helped to bake a cake, she scrubbed the kitchen table and she mopped the kitchen floor. She dusted the living room, and all the time they were working Aunt Aggie barely said a word. By the time they'd finished the chores the afternoon was almost over.

'Sit down,' said Aunt Aggie.

'I…I'm sorry,' Merryn whispered.

'So you should be,' snapped Aunt Aggie, 'and I've made a decision. I won't…'

Just then Hamish rushed in. He was bursting to tell about the things he'd seen. He chattered excitedly about sea anemones that could sting. Then he stopped and looked from Merryn to Aunt Aggie and back again. 'What's wrong?' he asked. 'Has something happened?'

Aunt Aggie shook her head as if she wasn't sure what to say. 'No,' she said at last. 'We had a disagreement, but it wasn't about anything important. I was so cross that I was going to stop you using the bedrooms, but you seem a lot happier so maybe I can give you one more chance.'

She turned to Merryn. 'Think yourself lucky that I've changed my mind. But what happened between us mustn't be repeated. Do I make myself clear?'

Merryn nodded. The argument and the reason for it weren't to be shared with Hamish. She didn't mind about that, but Aunt Aggie was wrong. It was important. It was more than important. It was so important that nothing else seemed to matter at all. Relieved that she could still get into the cubbyhole she followed Hamish upstairs. She swung the necklace between her finger and thumb. Then, growing bolder, she jiggled it in front of his face.

'Stop it,' he said. 'You're annoying me.'

Chuckling to herself, she went into her room. Aunt Aggie, Donald and Hamish had no idea that she was wearing the necklace. If Hamish had seen it she would have told him everything, but he hadn't, so the secret was hers alone.

Her smile faded suddenly. If the words in the note were true, the necklace would let her connect with magical beings. What kind of magical beings would they be? Fairies would be fun. Unicorns would be fantastic. But what if it meant scary beings like witches and giants? Shuddering at the thought, she grasped the necklace with both hands, pulled it off and put it back in the box.

'You must wear the necklace to save the horse,' said the voice.

It was obvious now. The horse was a magical being. That's why no-one else had heard it. Determinedly, she picked up the necklace and put it back on.

'Thank you,' said the voice. 'Now you must search the boxes, for inside them are things that might help you.'

She knelt in the corner next to the heap of old cardboard boxes. The lid of the largest box had a label. The writing on it said Merryn MacQueen - Shell Collection. She removed the lid and dug both hands into the shells. They trickled through her fingers, cowries, cockles, periwinkles and others that she couldn't name. But there was nothing to tell her how to save the horse so she closed the lid and moved it to one side.

The next box looked even older and there was no label. 'Yes!' she exclaimed as she opened it. For the things inside were like those in the necklace. The same smooth brown objects lay among a jumble of small stones. Like the pebbles on the beach, every stone was different, yet they all had one thing in common. Each one had a hole going right through it.

What were they, and why had Merryn collected them? She picked up one brown object and one stone, and ran across to Donald's cottage. Would he be able to see them? Or would they be invisible like the necklace? Holding them in her open palm she waited for him to say something.

'Well, well,' he said as he took them from her, 'sea-beans and hag-stones! It wouldn't surprise me if that invisible necklace was made with things like these.'

'It...' Merryn stopped herself just in time. 'Why do you think that?'

'Because people kept them as good luck charms,' he said. 'They were used to ward away witches, so it's likely that they'd be used in a magical necklace.' He gave the stone back to Merryn. 'That's a hag-stone. It's just a stone with a hole in it. The shape and size don't matter at all. The important thing is that the hole was made naturally. And this,' he said as he put the sea-bean into her hand, 'is a seed from a tropical tree. It's travelled all the way across the Atlantic Ocean.'

'Wow! Sea-beans and hag-stones,' she repeated. 'Sea-beans and hag-stones, sea-beans and hag-stones.'

She chanted the words all the way back to the cottage door. There was a pleasing rhythm to them. The names tripped off her tongue like a charm, but she remembered to stop singing before Aunt Aggie could hear her.

Chapter 6

After dinner, Aunt Aggie sent them out to the tent. 'I'm having an extra early night,' she said. 'You've quite worn me out and I don't want disturbing. So off you go.'

Merryn set her alarm and got into her sleeping bag. Her mind buzzed so much that she couldn't sleep. She lay with the necklace round her neck and a torch in her hand. Just after ten o'clock she must have dozed, for the next thing she knew, the alarm was beeping. She stopped it quickly, switched on her torch and got dressed.

Hamish turned towards her. 'What on earth are you doing?' he grumbled.

'I'm waiting for the horse to call.'

'You're bonkers,' he said. 'It won't call because there isn't one.' He gave an enormous yawn and turned over. 'Go back to sleep and don't wake me again.'

Merryn lay down on top of her sleeping bag. She switched off the torch and listened for a change in her brother's breathing. Not until she was sure he was asleep did she creep out of the tent.

As the hands on her watch reached midnight, the cry came again. It filled the air. It filled her head. It was the same as the night before. Only this time she was running, desperate to find the horse before it stopped calling. As she turned into a field the cry ended. A sudden eerie silence filled the air. She shivered and caught her breath. Anxiously she swung the torch beam, but she couldn't see a horse anywhere. Totally bewildered, she leaned against the gatepost and flashed the torch for one last time. That's when she saw it. Not the living breathing horse she'd expected, but an old wooden fencepost in the shape of a horse's head.

'It can't be,' she whispered. And yet she knew it was true. There was magic in the air. It crackled around her. It drew her towards the post and when she reached it, she knew what she had to do. She took off the necklace and slipped it over the wooden horse's head.

As soon as it left her hand it started to change. The thread began to grow. Breathlessly she watched as it stretched until it was two, four, six times its original length. The crackle in the air became more than sound. It was movement and colour. It was music of haunting beauty. It was a flurry of tiny sparks darting in every direction. They were filling the air around her. Then they were gathering round the post, twirling faster and faster until it was hidden in a whirl of rainbow threads.

As her eyes tried to follow their path Merryn grew dizzy. She stumbled and sat down, head bowed, eyes closed, her whole body spinning with the swirling sparks. Gradually the sensation passed. Something touched the back of her neck, something soft that breathed warm air. As she turned and looked up, the horse, for it truly was a horse, whinnied softly in welcome.

'I knew it,' she said as she jumped to her feet. 'I knew I wasn't dreaming. Only I don't know how...why...what you were doing inside a fence post.'

Across the sea on another island someone else had heard the horse's neigh. Week on week, year on year she had revelled in the sound. It travelled across the low-lying Reef of Tiree, speeding eastwards through channels of black magic. She laughed, rubbed her hands together gleefully and glanced at her clock. Setting the time by the horse's cry had become a midnight ritual. Times without number the plea for help had reached her, confirming that she still held the young stallion captive.

'Soon my new spell will break through his magic shield and destroy him forever,' she laughed. 'Just one more trial, and if that is successful, I'll go to Tiree and make an end of him.'

Hardly had the thought passed through her head before another sound reached her. It was a gentle sound, a whinny of welcome. She clapped her hands over her ears and sat down heavily. There must be white magic afoot. The horse was no longer asking for help. Help had arrived. And although she knew her magic was strong enough to send him back to the post before daybreak, she could not tell what spells could be unravelled between midnight and the rising of the sun.

There was no time to waste, but before she could leave, the spell had to be tested. Out she went to where a single tree stood on the hillside. She raised her arms above her head, directed all her destructive energy and shouted, 'Burn, burn, burn.'

Flames burst from every fingertip, and in one tremendous flare the tree was consumed. Nothing remained, not a charred twig, not a smouldering ember, *not even a speck of ash. Grinning with satisfaction, she took to the air.*

'He will not escape,' she said as she flew unerringly to the place where she had left him. 'Someone has seen through his wooden prison. I will discover who that person is, and I will destroy them both.'

Almost without realising what was happening Merryn found herself on the horse's back. As soon as she'd twisted her fingers through his mane he was heading out of the field and along the track. Like the wind he went, across the dunes and on to the long sandy stretch of Traigh nan Gilean.

He cantered along the edge of the waves and she laughed with joy as the spray flew like silver sparks in the moonlight. She could have gone on riding for ever, but all too soon the horse slowed to a walk. At the end of the beach he turned into a tiny cove and passed along a narrow passageway between high rocks. Above the high tide line he stopped, pawed the ground and looked back at her. He was telling her to dig. He didn't need words. His meaning was as clear as if he'd spoken.

She slid from his back, knelt down and pushed her fingers into the dry sand. She dug and dug, throwing sea-smoothed pebbles aside, wondering all the while what she was seeking. She'd almost given up hope of finding anything when her fingers found something soft. Pulling out a bundle she looked up at the horse.

'What shall I do?' she asked. It was a pointless question because she already knew the answer. It was as if she'd always known. She unrolled the fabric and there was a sporran attached to a belt. She tried to open it, but there didn't seem to be a fastener of any kind. Was this it? Was this all the horse wanted? Puzzled, she passed the belt round her waist and buckled it. Then she folded up the cloth and stuffed it in the pocket of her fleece.

The horse pawed the ground. He looked up at the sky. He turned his head this way and that. His nostrils flared. He shook his mane and broke into a panic-stricken whinny. Something was spooking him. He was telling her to get on his back. As soon as she mounted, he was away, galloping even faster than before, his thundering hooves making deep prints in the damp sand. Over the dunes he went, and in a very short time he was back beside the wooden fence post.

'Why? Why have you brought me here? I want to go to the cottage. I want to prove to Hamish that I wasn't dreaming.'

The horse bucked and reared. He nudged the post with his nose. His meaning was clear. He had to return to the place where she'd found him.

'No,' she choked on a sob. 'You can't go back. I saved you. You've got to stay.'

She tried to pull him away from the post, but he took her sleeve between his teeth and pulled her back. She put her hands on each side of his face and looked into his eyes. Although he shed no tears it was as if he was crying too. He shook his head so that the necklace rattled. He was telling her to take it back. He was telling her of danger.

'I can't,' she cried. 'Now I've found you, I can't let you go.'

Even as she spoke, her hands reached out towards the necklace. She fought to hold them back, but they were caught in the magic spell. Unable to stop herself, she slipped the necklace from his neck onto her own.

The colours that swirled round them were no longer bright and glittering. They were dark and murky like the waters of a stagnant pool. The sound that accompanied them was so mournful that it made her weep all the more. She wrinkled her nose and tried not to breathe in the smell of things that had been long dead. She was forced back as a cloud of filthy vapour rose from the ground. It enveloped the horse. It swirled and disappeared into the wooden post, and when the last wisp had vanished, the horse had vanished too.

Chapter 7

'Come back,' Merryn cried. 'You must come back.' She pulled off the necklace and threw it over the post.

'Please, come back.'

Nothing happened. No colours came to brighten the sky. No music came to fill the air. No coloured threads swirled round the post and the horse did not reappear. Filled with despair she put the necklace back round her own neck, flung her arms round the wooden post and wept. She'd failed. She hadn't saved the horse at all. She slid to the ground wondering if she would ever see him again.

Time passed. As the night grew cooler she struggled to her feet and stared at the post. That's all it was, an old wooden fence post, grey with age, gnarled and twisted into the rough shape of a horse's head. Her hand reached out and stroked the length of the wooden nose. Had it really turned into a living, breathing horse? Or had it been a dream?

Her fingers flew to the necklace. It was still round her neck. If it really had grown to fit the horse, then it had shrunk again. It was too impossible to be true. Sadly, with a last lingering look at the post she turned and walked away.

But what was that? A distant roaring filled the air. It grew louder and louder. She slammed her hands over her ears and fell to her knees as a funnel of black wind came rushing out of the sky. It was heading for the wooden horse and she could do nothing to stop it. Her scream cut through the roar of the wind. She clenched her fists and tensed her body as she waited for the crash. No crash came. At the very last moment the black whirling shape slowed and stopped. It was no longer a wind. It was a woman, a woman in a black flowing cloak, a woman mounted on a broomstick.

'A witch,' she gasped. Shaking with fear she crouched behind the clumps of grass and rushes.

'Now my fine foe,' snarled the witch. 'Prepare to meet your doom. Dumb you may be, but deaf you are not, and I tell you this. The magic that released you will not release you again. I will put an end to it. I will destroy you and I will destroy the person who tried to save you.'

Merryn's hand flew to her mouth. She chewed on her knuckles. All her thoughts were blanked out by the terror that gripped her. All she could do was watch, listen and wait to see what the witch would do.

'First I will deal with you,' said the witch. She dropped her broomstick and stamped round the post uttering a string of strange words. Chanted in a droning monotone they had neither rhyme nor rhythm. They blended together and ended abruptly as the witch raised both hands and pointed at the wooden horse's head.

'Burn,' she shouted, 'burn, burn, burn.'

Flames shot from her fingertips. Straight as arrows they flew through the air and hit the post. A scream rose in Merryn's throat. She clamped her hand over her mouth to deaden the sound. Flames engulfed the post. They flickered high into the air. They lit the sky. Not bearing to watch, Merryn closed her eyes. Tears streamed down her cheeks. Her body shook with sobs for the loss of the horse and for the terrible way his life had ended.

'Burn, I said burn,' screamed the witch. 'Why will you not burn?'

Merryn, hearing the witch's words, looked up. Her heart leapt when she saw that the post was still there and the fire was no longer burning.

The witch tore her hair. She looked up, raised her arms above her head and screamed. 'What magic is this that breaks my spells? Lead me to its source. Help me to destroy it.'

Merryn's heart froze inside her chest. Was the witch calling on some even greater power? Would other witches arrive? Anxiously she looked round for signs of rushing winds and flying broomsticks.

Thankfully, nothing came to disturb the sky.

The witch began to move, an ungainly dance of leaps, hops and jumps, of thrusting fists and jerking elbows.

'Widdershins, widdershins,' she cried as she circled the post in an anti-clockwise direction. 'Unwind the spell that douses flame.' On and on she went, dancing her crazy dance and repeating the words over and over.

Merryn clutched the necklace as she watched the witch with frightened eyes. 'No,' she whispered. 'No, no, no.' And she didn't stop whispering until the witch fell silent.

For the second time the witch raised her arms and pointed at the post. 'Burn,' she ordered. 'Burn, burn, burn.'

'Don't burn, don't burn, don't burn,' Merryn chanted under her breath.

But as the witch thrust her hands towards the post, flames flew from her fingertips. They flashed and flared. They licked the post, but within seconds they flickered, fizzled and died.

The witch stared at her hands. She shook her head as if she couldn't believe that her spell had failed. 'Curse you,' she cried, 'and curse the one who interferes with my spells. As long as there's breath in my body and blood in my veins you'll never be free.'

In a fit of fury she lifted her broomstick and brought it crashing down between the wooden horse's ears. Again and again she struck. 'Take that and that and that,' she yelled. 'I'll bruise your body. I'll break your bones. I may not kill you but I'll make sure you never stand again.'

'Please stop. Please stop,' Merryn mouthed the words. She winced at every thwack of the broomstick as if she too was feeling the pain. 'Please stop.'

The witch did not stop. She went on striking the horse until the thud of wood on wood changed to the sound of splintering. Triumphantly she raised her hand. 'At last I've made my mark.'

She walked all round the post, peering at it closely. Her hands ran over it. Round and round she went, searching high, searching low. Her fingers flew faster and faster over the wooden horse's head, down his nose, round his ears, along his neck.

'What?' she screamed. 'No split, no splinter? I heard it crack. It must be broken.'

She stopped, picked up her broomstick and examined it closely. 'Not my broomstick,' she wailed. 'I can't have broken my broomstick.' Turning her back on the wooden post, she sat astride the shaft. 'Fly' she commanded. 'Show me you can still fly.'

Merryn watched as the broomstick faltered. It was obviously struggling as it rose and fell in a jerking motion.

'Curses, curses,' screamed the witch as it swerved and dropped her to the ground.

The witch lay still. Merryn let out a long shaky breath and stood up. This should have been her chance to run away, but the witch was already struggling to her feet. Merryn dropped down again and watched as the witch untied a cord from round her waist.

'Stupid, stupid,' the witch muttered as she began to bind the cord around the broomstick shaft. 'Why was I so stupid?'

Merryn could do nothing. The witch was facing her and she daren't move for fear of drawing attention to her hiding place. For several minutes the witch wound the cord round the broomstick. With each turn of her hand she chanted. 'Mend broomstick, mend.'

Merryn gritted her teeth and made up a whispered chant of her own. 'Don't mend. Don't mend.'

The witch went on winding. Then all of a sudden she stopped and gave a triumphant cry. She dropped the broomstick and stared at the ground.

'Aha!' she said. 'There are bent rushes here. There are footprints in the dew.'

She started to move along the trail of flattened grasses that Merryn had left. She pointed her long nose towards Merryn and sniffed so loudly that Merryn shuddered at the sound.

'Aha!' the witch said again. 'I smell the disgustingly sweet smell of white magic. I smell ...'

Merryn didn't wait to hear more. She leapt to her feet and ran.

Chapter 8

Gasping for breath, Merryn rushed into the tent. 'Wake up, Hamish. We've got to get out of here.' She grabbed him by the shoulders and tried to drag him out of his sleeping bag.

Hamish pushed her away. 'Get off. I'm not going anywhere. Leave me alone.'

She grabbed him again, but Hamish pushed her so hard that she fell over. Sobbing with fear and frustration she pleaded with him.

'Get up. The witch is coming. If she catches me she'll kill me.'

Slowly, Hamish sat up. He switched on his torch and stared at Merryn.

'Switch it off,' she yelled. 'I told you, the witch is coming. If she sees a light she'll know where I am. It isn't safe. Please, get up and come into the cottage.'

Hamish didn't switch off the torch. Its beam shone out like a beacon, waving this way and that as Merryn tried to snatch it from him.

'You've got to stop this.' Hamish dropped the torch and caught hold of her hands. 'You've had another nightmare. First it was a horse. Now it's a witch. You're awake now. Forget them both. There isn't a horse and there isn't a witch either.'

The witch followed the person who had run so swiftly away. The broomstick would not fly so she hobbled along the track. By the time she reached the cottage she was exhausted. Panting for breath she leaned against the gate to plan her next move. Whoever brought the horse to life had to be eliminated. But which spell should she use? Each one relied on knowing something about her victim and so far she knew very little. She scratched her head and tried to remember what she'd seen. There'd been a glimpse of long hair flying, so presumably it was a girl. But how could a mere girl have broken a spell that had held the horse captive for so many years?

Should she go into the cottage and face her? She gloated over the methods she could use to make the girl reveal the secret of her power. It would be satisfying to make her suffer before she got rid of her for good. On the other hand, if the girl's magic proved to be really strong, it would be risky. There may be a long battle ahead and she was already desperate for rest. The quickest solution would be to burn the cottage with the girl inside.

She raised her hands ready to invoke the spell, but at that moment a light began to flash. It shone out, piercing the sky, dipping to sweep along the grass then rising to run along the cottage walls. For a moment it caught her in its beam, shining directly into her eyes. She fell to her knees, shielded her eyes against the brightness and crawled cautiously towards its source.

But what was this? Something was barring her way. Although she could see nothing she could go no farther. She stood up and pushed the invisible barrier with all her might. It moved a little under her hands, but as soon as she let go it bounced back again. She could neither move it aside nor force her way through it.

'I must find a way,' she fumed. 'My life depends on it.'

Terrified as she was, Merryn had to know what was happening. She peered through the tent flap and recoiled in horror.

'What am I going to do?' she wailed.

'Come to your senses, I hope,' said Hamish. 'Just get it into your head that there isn't a witch.'

'But there is,' Merryn insisted. 'If you don't believe me come and look.'

Hamish refused to move. Merryn turned away in exasperation. The witch was standing a few metres from the tent. She was moving her hands in front of her face as if she was feeling something. Then she took a few steps backwards and raised her hands.

'Burn, burn,' she cried as a flurry of flames left her fingertips.

'Don't burn, don't burn,' Merryn screamed.

The flames flickered and rose high into the air but they stopped short of the tent. They arched over the top of it and ran down the other side.

'It's all right,' Merryn gasped. 'She can't do it. She couldn't burn the horse and she can't burn the tent. There's something blocking her.'

The witch stamped her feet. She cursed and called down spell after spell, but nothing worked. Merryn laughed with relief and went out of the tent to face her.

Hamish followed. 'See,' he said. 'I told you. There's no-one there.'

He flashed his torch across the lawn and Merryn saw the witch raise her arm to protect herself. Grabbing the torch from Hamish, Merryn shone it directly into the witch's eyes.

'Argh!' The witch turned her head away. 'You win this time,' she snarled, 'but I'll be back. I'll beat you yet.'

With a shake of her fist she hobbled away, muttering as she went.

'She's gone. The witch has gone. I won. I won.'

Merryn danced up and down until Hamish caught her by the arm and forced her into the tent. He made her sit down and then he placed a hand on her forehead.

'You don't feel hot,' he said, 'but I reckon you have a fever. You're... what's the word for seeing things that aren't there?'

'Hallucinating,' said Merryn, 'only that's not what I'm doing. The witch really was there. She's gone but she'll be back. She said she'd make an end of me and I've got to find out how to stop her.'

'No you don't,' said Hamish. 'It was just a dream. There isn't a witch. I looked and I couldn't see a thing.'

Muttering angrily the witch struggled back to her broomstick. The cord had unravelled and she began to bind it all over again. When it was as tight as she could make it, she sat astride and ordered it to fly. It quivered and lurched and rose a little way into the air.

'Higher,' she yelled. 'Fly higher.'

It was no use. It flew so low that her feet trailed on the ground. Her shoes scraped along rocks and dipped into puddles. Each time they came to a fence she had to squeeze through the strands of wire, and every time they came to a wall she had to scramble over. Getting more and more frustrated she guided the struggling broomstick to her retreat in the long-forgotten souterrain.

Sunrise came just as she arrived. There was no time to collect fresh heather for a bed. Exhausted, she squeezed through the narrow entrance and dropped into the stone-lined chamber. She pulled off her sodden shoes, flopped down and tried to sleep. But sleep would not come. Her mind, running over the events of the night, kept her awake. The burning spell had only failed because someone had re-awakened the old magic. Yet how could that be? For years she had seen no sign of Selkies, Fairy Folk, or mortals with The Gift. She had thought them dead and gone forever.

'Ill luck to the one who stands in my way,' she cursed.

'I could sense the sea-beans and hag- stones. But there must be something even more powerful. It would take more than sea-beans and hag-stones to stop my spell.'

Still unable to sleep, she tried again to bind the broomstick. 'I need willow bark,' she fumed. 'This can only be a temporary measure.' She kept on trying to mend the broomstick, but however tightly she wound the cord, the split would not close.

'Without you I'm useless,' she complained. 'I shouldn't have used you to thrash the horse, I know that now and I'm sorry, but that alone shouldn't stop you from mending.'

She struggled for an explanation. Perhaps the girl's magic had lodged in the post and rubbed off onto the broomstick. Mending a broomstick was always difficult. With white magic working against her it seemed to be impossible. She needed to buy a new one, but that would mean flying across the sea. That was impossible too. The broomstick was too weak to embark on such a perilous journey.

Determinedly she got to her feet. 'I'll make a new on,' she said. 'Then I'll tackle that interfering girl once and for *all. She only beat me because I was unprepared. Tonight I'll be ready. She will not beat me again.'*

Merryn was in tears. She'd tried her best to make Hamish believe in the witch, but she couldn't convince him.

'You imagined it. Or else it was a dream. You'd have to be crazy to believe you saw a witch on a broomstick. I don't believe you, so stop talking rubbish.'

Too tired to argue, she put her head on the pillow. It didn't matter how scared she was, she'd have to face the witch on her own.

'OK,' she said, 'I won't say another word.'

'Good, because I'm going to sleep,' said Hamish. 'Do me a favour and forget it.'

Merryn knew that she would never forget. However long she lived she'd remember everything that had happened. She'd remember the terror of seeing the witch. But more than that, she'd remember the ride along the edge of the sea, the velvet softness of the horse's nose, the warmth of his breath and the look in his sad, brown eyes. He was a magical being, but he was more real than any horse she'd ever ridden. She tried to push the image of the witch out of her head, but it was still there when she closed her eyes. It refused to go away. It kept her awake for most of the night, and when she slept, it invaded her dreams.

Chapter 9

The witch winced as she got up from her bed. Walking to the cottage had given her blisters. The thought of going out to search for wood was unbearable, but she had no choice. Without her broomstick she had been unable to catch the wretched girl. And if the horse was released again, she would have to follow him and find another way of ending his life for ever. Yes, a new broomstick had to be her top priority. She tried to remember where there were trees on Tiree, but she knew they were few and far between. She peered out of the souterrain, shielded her eyes against the early morning sun and squinted angrily at the cloudless sky.

'Mist,' she cried, 'block out the sun. I can't bear the light.'

She opened her mouth and a thick mist poured out of it. It rolled across the grass, spread rapidly over the island and reduced visibility to no more than a metre. Hoping that the ailing broomstick would not fail completely, she mounted and flew slowly along the single track road. She lifted her feet as high as she was able, but from time to time, they scraped the ground. It was an ordeal, but it was better than trying to walk on feet that were already blistered.

Mile after mile she travelled, her eyes piercing the mist, searching, yet failing to find a single tree. Eventually she came across a group of wind-stunted willows, but their trunks were slender. She hacked and stripped until she'd gathered enough bark for binding the

twigs to the shaft. Reluctantly she lifted her aching limbs
back onto the broomstick, and set out, hoping to find birch
twigs and an ash branch.

In the moments before Merryn climbed out of her
sleeping bag she went over the events of the night.
Everything that had happened was far too vivid to
have been imagined. And yet, the more she thought
about it, the more incredible it seemed. Had she really
run away from a witch? Had she really released a
horse from an old wooden fencepost? And had he
really taken her to find a sporran? Fully awake now,
her hands felt for it. It was still fastened round her
waist. It was real, and luckily it was hidden because
just then the tent flap was pulled aside.

'Get a move on,' said Aunt Aggie. 'I shouldn't have
to remind you that breakfast is at seven. Hurry up and
come indoors. There's been a change in the weather. I
don't understand it at all. One minute the sky was blue
and the next it was lost in the thickest mist I've ever
seen. It's not a morning for venturing out, so you'll
have to amuse yourselves indoors.

'Can't I even go to the beach?' asked Hamish.

'Certainly not,' said Aunt Aggie. 'You'd be lost
before you got to the gate. You'll have to wait until it
clears.'

Hamish left the tent mumbling unhappily. Merryn
had so many things to think about that she didn't mind
staying in at all. As soon as Aunt Aggie and Hamish
had left the tent, she unbuckled the belt and pushed
the sporran down to the bottom of her sleeping bag.

All through breakfast her mind refused to think of

anything else. The minute the washing up was finished she rushed back to the tent.

For a moment she wondered if Hamish was right, if it really had been a dream. What if the sporran wasn't there? Grabbing the sleeping bag with both hands she held it upside down and shook it.

'Yes!' Out fell the sporran and the belt. She fastened the belt around her waist and pulled her fleece over the sporran. Then she went up to her bedroom to take a closer look. When she'd first seen them in the moonlight, and when she'd hidden them so hurriedly, she hadn't realised how beautiful they were. Made of rich brown leather, they were as polished and shiny as a new conker. But although she turned the sporran over and over, she couldn't find a way of opening it. Her breath caught in her throat as she recognised the pattern that was embossed on it. It was the same as the one on the wooden box. It was the pattern that has neither beginning nor end.

'It must be a magic symbol,' she whispered, 'only I don't know what it means.'

As she traced her finger along its intricate line the door began to open. Quickly she thrust the sporran behind her back and faced Hamish with a scowl.

'You're supposed to knock.'

Hamish grinned. 'Sorry. I forgot. You don't usually mind. Have you got a secret or something?

'Yes I have,' she said. 'I tried to share it with you only you wouldn't listen.'

'Well I'm listening now.' He dashed across the room, threw himself on the bed and tried to pull her arms from behind her back.

'You're hiding something. I know you are. Come on, show me.'

'Get off, Hamish. There's no need to start a fight.' She pushed him away, and held up the belt and sporran. 'Look, isn't it amazing.'

Hamish frowned. He stared at her hands. His mouth opened but no words came out.

'Come on,' she said as she waved the sporran in front of him. 'Here, take hold of it. The horse showed me where it was hidden. He took me for a ride. Then the witch came and tried to burn him. Well, not exactly him, but the wooden post he went back into.'

She stopped when she saw that Hamish was shaking his head as if he couldn't believe a word she was saying.

'You're crazy,' he said. 'You're talking rubbish. I haven't a clue what you're on about.'

'Remember,' she said. 'I woke you up last night because the witch chased me. She tried to burn the tent. You said it was a bad dream, only it wasn't.' She thrust the sporran towards him. 'It was real and this proves it.'

'The only thing it proves,' said Hamish, 'is that it was a dream. I can't see anything so I don't know what you think you're holding.'

Merryn closed her eyes as the truth suddenly dawned. Of course, it was simple. Hamish didn't believe in the witch because he hadn't seen her. She'd been carried away on a wave of enthusiasm. She'd forgotten that she was the only one with The Gift. That's why she could see the necklace, the horse, the witch and the sporran. There was no point in trying to tell Hamish anything. He didn't have The Gift. He couldn't see the sporran. No wonder he thought she was crazy.

'Stop. Please don't go,' she said as he walked towards the door. 'Let me explain. I know it's hard to believe. I didn't believe it myself at first. Come on, Hamish. Let me share it with you. Please.'

He paused and looked at her. 'The thing is, I'd love to share it. It sounds great, horses and witches and magic and all that. Only there isn't anything to share. You really are crazy. You say you're holding something but your hands are empty. You've got me worried and I don't know what to do. You need to see a doctor. I'm going to tell Aunt Aggie.'

Merryn dropped the sporran on the bed and chased after him. 'Don't, don't you dare tell Aunt Aggie anything,' she yelled. 'I was holding a sporran. I'm telling the truth. It's there on the bed.'

Grabbing him by the arm she pulled him back into the room. He punched her with his free hand and broke away from her grasp. He walked across to the bed, stared and shook his head. 'I thought…no. I told you, there's nothing there.'

'Hamish, please,' she said, 'let me explain. I'm not making it up. Honestly I'm not. Why won't you believe me?'

'Because it's too crazy to be true,' he said, 'but I won't tell Aunt Aggie and I won't run away. I promise. Just get hold of me. Please. I want to try something.'

She grasped his arm.

He looked up at her and grinned. 'Now let go.'

As she released him he reached towards the sporran. He tried to pick it up, but his fingers passed straight through it. He rubbed his eyes with his fists.

'I thought I saw something,' he said. 'It was only for a moment, but I couldn't feel it. I must have imagined it. I think I'm going crazy too.'

'No, you're not. It was the sporran. You saw it. I know you did. Try again, please.'

As he moved his hand across the duvet, she watched his fingers pass through the sporran. To him, there was nothing there, yet to her it was as real as everything else in the room.

He scratched his head and rubbed his eyes again. 'I don't know what's going on, but there's definitely something odd. Touch me.'

She reached out and took hold of his arm.

His eyes grew wide as he stared at the bed. 'Let go. Now touch me.' As he picked up the sporran his face broke into a grin.

Merryn burst into tears.

'It's all right,' he said. 'Don't get upset. I can see it now.'

'I'm not upset,' she sobbed. 'I'm relieved. It was horrible when you said I'd been dreaming, and it was even worse when you said I was crazy. It's magic, real magic. There is a horse and there's a witch too, honestly.'

'I believe you now,' he said. 'I don't understand it, but there must be something that lets you see the magic. Then when you touch me, it lets me see it too. You'd better tell me all about it.'

Chapter 10

'Thank goodness you believe me,' said Merryn. 'I know it's hard to understand. I don't even understand it myself. All I know is that I have something called The Gift. Our great-great-great-great-grandmother had it. And guess what? Her name was the same as mine. She was Merryn MacQueen too. She had The Gift and she passed it on to me.'

She took hold of the necklace. 'Then I found this. It's made of sea-beans and hag-stones. They guard against witches and other evil creatures. I think that's why the witch couldn't reach me.'

'I can't see it,' said Hamish. He took hold of her arm and his eyes widened. 'Gosh! It's like the sporran I can only see it when we're touching.'

Merryn put her arm round his shoulders, took off the necklace and let him hold it. He ran his fingers over the sea-beans and hag-stones while she told him everything that had happened.

'I can hardly believe it,' he said when she'd finished. 'It's like the wardrobe and Narnia, or finding Platform nine and three quarters and going to Hogwarts.'

'Sort of,' she said, 'only they're just stories and this is real. It's truly happening and it's a mystery. We've no idea what's going to happen next. We haven't a clue how it's going to end.'

She paused as a shudder ran across her shoulders. 'We don't even know if we'll live to tell the tale. And something else is puzzling me. Why can't I open the sporran and why would a horse have a sporran anyway?'

'You can't open it because it's private,' he said, 'and it doesn't belong to the horse. It belongs to the horse's owner. I reckon it's a man because if it was a woman she'd have a handbag.'

Merryn looked at the sporran thoughtfully. It was an obvious explanation yet it didn't satisfy her. 'No, she said, 'a man would have a bigger one, and he'd need a bigger horse too.'

'Then it must belong to a boy.'

'Oh! No!' Merryn folded her arms and scowled. 'I don't want him to belong to anyone, least of all a boy. I thought if I saved him, I'd be able to keep him.'

'Don't talk daft,' he said. 'If it's as real as you say it is, it must belong to someone. Besides, you haven't saved it yet, and even if you do, you can't take it on the plane when we leave.'

'I suppose not,' Merryn said. 'I just didn't think I was rescuing him for a horrible, smelly boy.'

Immediately the words were spoken, she felt ashamed. She'd been chosen. She'd promised to help, and for the horse's sake she would keep her promise.

'But if it does belong to a boy, he'd better be a nice one. And I'd like to know who he is and why he needs me to save his horse. I don't see why he can't save it for himself.'

Hamish shrugged. 'Maybe he isn't on Tiree.'

Deep in thought, Merryn picked up the sporran and tried to imagine the person who usually wore it. She closed her eyes and wished with all her might that it would tell her what to do. A moment passed before her eyes opened in surprise. Something was happening. Something was changing. The sporran was growing heavier.

'There's something inside,' she said, 'and I'm sure it wasn't there before.'

Hamish nudged her. 'Open it. Only hang on a minute.' He linked his arm through hers. 'I want to see what it is.'

'I can't,' she said. 'I can't find a fastener.'

No sooner had she spoken than the sporran opened itself. Immediately the room was bathed in light, a mystical light that glowed and shimmered. Not daring to put her fingers inside the sporran, she carefully upended it. Three crystals, purple, pink and yellow slid gently onto the bed. Each one sent out a beam of light. Each beam passed through the other crystals. Lines of purple, pink and yellow joined together to weave a figure of eight that crossed through the purple crystal.

'Wow,' they exclaimed together.

'Look at the pattern they're making,' said Merryn. 'It's a magic symbol, I'm sure it is. It hasn't got a beginning or an end. It goes on and on for ever.'

Her hand moved of its own accord. It hovered over the crystals. The pink one pulled her towards it. She picked it up and held it in her palm.

'Your turn,' she whispered.

'Can I have the purple one?'

Merryn shrugged. 'I don't think you get to choose. The pink one chose me. Just put your hand over them and see what happens.'

Hamish stretched out his hand and picked up the yellow crystal. 'It's tingling all the way up my arm,' he squealed. 'Something's changed. I feel sort of sparkly inside. I tried to get the purple one only it wouldn't let me. It must be meant for someone else.'

'I bet it's for the owner of the horse,' said Merryn, 'and maybe it'll help us to find him.'

Hamish held up his crystal and pranced across the room. The figure of eight grew larger as the colours went with him. Merryn left the purple crystal on the bed. She held up the pink one. Hamish raised and lowered his arms. Merryn joined in and they danced round the room. No matter what they did, the figure of eight never faltered. Sometimes one loop was bigger than the other, but the lines always crossed through the purple crystal. They giggled and squealed, and Hamish whooped with joy.

The door opened and in stormed Aunt Aggie. 'What on earth do you think you're doing?' she shouted. 'I warned you. I warned you both.'

Merryn closed her fist over the pink crystal. Hamish flinched and pushed the yellow crystal into his pocket. Merryn covered the purple crystal with her hand. Even though all three crystals were hidden, the colours went on weaving their figure of eight.

Aunt Aggie looked from Merryn to Hamish. She shook her head and made a tutting sound with her tongue. 'You're lucky that Donald came to see me just now,' she said. 'He seems to think that you're bright, intelligent children with perfect manners. I can't see it myself but he reckons I'm being too strict. Maybe I am. He has grandchildren so I suppose he should know. But I won't have you bouncing about. If you want to leap around you'll have to wait for the mist to lift. Once you're outside you can leap as much as you like, but I will not have it in the house.'

Hamish was the first to speak. 'I'm sorry, Aunt Aggie,' he said. 'I won't do it again. I promise.'

'I'm sorry too,' said Merryn. 'We forgot.'

'Well don't forget again,' said Aunt Aggie. 'I thought the ceiling was going to come down. It's lucky for you that nothing fell off the dresser.'

She looked out of the window. 'Maybe the mist will lift and you'll be able to go out later. Now I'll make lunch while you get on with your homework, and remember what I said, no more bouncing about.'

They waited until the door closed and Aunt Aggie's footsteps had died away.

'Phew! That was close,' said Hamish.

'It was fine,' said Merryn as she put her pink crystal next to the purple one. 'She couldn't see a thing. And wasn't that kind of Donald? We must remember to thank him.'

'I wish we could stay with him,' said Hamish. 'It would be much more fun and I could look at his books whenever I wanted.'

He examined his crystal and his face broke into a grin. 'I've just realised something. You're not touching me. You haven't been touching me for ages and I can still see the crystals. I can see the necklace too, and the sporran. My crystal must have given me some power of my own.'

He started to punch the air with his fists. 'I've got magic power. I've got...'

'Shush,' said Merryn, 'or Aunt Aggie will hear you.'

Hamish stopped. 'I can't help it. I've got magic power and I want everyone to know. I'm going to tell mum and dad when they phone.'

'Don't you dare,' Merryn snapped. 'It's got to be a secret.'

'I don't see why.' His smile turned to a frown. 'I've got to tell somebody. I'll burst if I don't.' He turned towards the door. 'I'm going to tell Aunt Aggie then she'll understand why we were bouncing about.'

Merryn pushed past him and blocked the door. 'No, you won't. She doesn't believe in magic. If she thinks we're getting mixed up in it she'll send us away.'

He looked at his crystal and sighed. 'It's the best thing I've ever had. People are always telling us to share. Now I've got something worth sharing, you won't let me. It seems mean keeping it to myself. I don't see why I can't tell.'

'It's because we don't know who's out there,' said Merryn. 'There's at least one witch and there may be more. They might have spies. They might even be disguised as ordinary people. If they know where our magic power comes from they'll be able to destroy it. If that happens we won't be able to save the horse and the witch will kill us. It's got to be a secret. You've got to promise not to tell anyone.'

Chapter 11

Merryn watched the magical line of light winding between the crystals. On and on it went, always in a figure of eight, always following a path without an end. She forced her eyes away from the hypnotic effect, picked up the sporran and tried to find the opening. It had completely disappeared.

'I don't understand,' she said. 'I've been told to save the horse, but I don't know how to do it. I thought the sporran might have a message inside. Something or someone will have to tell me what to do.'

For the second time, the sporran opened itself and something leapt out onto the bed. Hamish squealed and picked it up.

'It's a teeny tiny book,' he said, 'and we're going to need this.' He pulled a magnifying glass out of his pocket and peered at the writing on the cover.

'We can't read it,' he said. 'It's in a foreign language and we can't ask anyone to help because they won't be able to see it. We're stumped.' He flopped down on Merryn's bed and closed his eyes. 'I can't read it. I give up.'

Merryn brought the words into focus and looked at the elaborate golden curlicues. 'I don't even recognise the letters but I'm not giving up for anything.' She gave an exasperated sigh. 'I want to save the horse, but I can't do it without help. Please, somebody, show me how to read it.'

Immediately the book began to grow. She watched, open-mouthed as it grew to the same size as her diary. The golden letters began to move. The curlicues undid themselves and formed new letters, capital letters that she could read.

KESTER'S BOOK

'Look,' her voice rose in amazement. 'It belongs to someone called Kester and the pattern round the edge is the one that never ends.'

She stared as something began to appear in the centre of the cover. It was just like the picture she'd drawn in the dust on top of the chest. It was a horse's head in a circle. The only difference was that her name didn't appear underneath it.

Hamish snatched the book from her. 'Never mind the cover. What does it say inside?' He flicked through the pages. 'It's blank,' he said. 'I don't believe it. Every single page is blank.'

'It can't be.' Merryn snatched it back. She went through it from beginning to end. Then she started at the end and went back to the beginning. Hamish was right. There wasn't so much as a word.

'I told you,' said Hamish. 'It's hopeless. We're stumped.'

'Don't say that,' said Merryn. 'Maybe it's written in invisible ink.'

'That doesn't help. If it's invisible we can't read it, and if we can't read it we're still stumped. It's a wild goose, or rather a wild horse chase.' He laughed as if he'd said something really clever. 'Get it! Wild horse chase!'

Merryn gave him a push. 'Stop it, Hamish. Of course I get it, but it isn't funny. If you're going to make silly jokes I'll be better off without you. If you think we're stumped you can leave me to work it out by myself.'

Hamish pushed her back. 'Just because you're older than me doesn't mean you can tell me what to do. I don't care what you say, I'm going to see what Aunt Aggie thinks...'

A sudden rustling of pages stopped him in mid-sentence. Merryn watched as the book opened itself and letters began to appear. She read out the words as they wrote themselves across the page.

'Breathe no word of what you know.
Breathe no word of what you've seen.
Place your hand upon this book and
swear to keep its secrets.'

'You're kidding,' said Hamish. 'You're making it up.'

'I'm not.' She passed the book to him. 'Here, see for yourself.'

Hamish looked. He dropped the book and backed away. 'It's spooky. I don't like it and I'm not going to promise anything.' He grabbed the door handle ready to leave. 'It won't move,' he gasped. His voice rose in panic. 'I can't get out, Merryn. I can't get out.'

'Be quiet or Aunt Aggie will hear you.' Merryn elbowed him out of the way. 'I'll open it if you promise not to tell. Do you promise? Cross your heart and hope to die.'

Hamish nodded. 'OK. I promise. Just let me out.'

'You'd better mean it.' She tried to turn the handle, but it wouldn't move. Her stomach churned as she stepped back. She chewed on her fingers as she wondered what to do. Hamish was right about it being spooky. They were trapped. If they wanted to get out, they would have to do as the book told them.

'Put your hand on the book and swear,' she insisted. 'Then I think it'll let you out.'

Hamish slumped on the floor. 'I'm not touching it. How do I know I can trust it? It might be a trick.'

Maybe he was right. Hoping for some different instructions Merryn picked up the book. The message was the same, but now the words were in capitals, and as she watched, a thick black line appeared underneath them.

'Please promise,' she said. 'If you don't we could be stuck in here for ever.'

Hamish groaned. 'But if Aunt Aggie can't get us out she'll call the police,'

Merryn sat down on the floor and tried to reason with him. 'The door locked itself because you said you'd tell Aunt Aggie. If you promise not to tell, I bet you'll be able to open it. I can't open it and no-one else can, not Aunt Aggie, not even the police. You're the only one who can do it.'

'But it could still be a trick, couldn't it?'

'I don't think so,' she said. 'If you'd seen the horse and the witch you'd know which one to trust. But look, something's happening to the book.' She watched as new words began to form.

'You'd better read this. It's another message, and it's definitely for you.' She held the book in front of his face. 'Look, it says Hamish.'

Hamish flinched. 'That makes it even spookier. How does it know my name? Take it away. I don't want to see any more.'

'You haven't got a choice,' said Merryn. 'It won't let you go until you've read it.'

Hamish rubbed his eyes and buried his head in his hands. 'I don't want to read it. I don't even want to look at it. I don't want anything to do with your stupid horse, or your stupid witch, or your stupid magic.'

Merryn put her arm round his shoulders. 'It's not as bad as you think. All you have to do is promise not to tell. You don't have to help if you don't want to. I'll do it all by myself. Come on, Hamish. Read it. Please'

Hamish pushed her away and wiped his nose on his sleeve.

'Ugh!' Merryn turned up her nose in disgust, but she resisted the urge to tell him off. She just held the book so that he could see the words for himself.

Hamish
From the moment you picked up the yellow
crystal you became part of the Quest.
However, there is still time to back out.
If that is your choice,
you will forget everything that has happened.
You will lose the power to see the magic.
But consider this.
The road ahead is a dangerous one.
Your sister needs your help.
You can make all the difference.
If you continue,
you must not shirk the challenges I set.
You must promise to keep everything secret
and you must keep going to the very end.

Chapter 12

When Hamish read the message in Kester's Book his face turned pale and he began to shake.

'It's OK,' said Merryn. 'You don't have to help. I'll manage by myself. I'm the one who heard the horse. You can back out now, if that's what you want.'

Hamish buried his face in his hands. There was a long pause. 'I can't,' he said. 'I can't let you do it on your own. But how can I promise to do things when I don't even know what they are? Besides I don't think I can keep a secret.'

No sooner had Hamish expressed his doubts than the invisible pen began to write again. It was as if the book had ears.

Hamish
If you doubt your ability to keep a secret
I can stop your words
each time you think to speak of the magic.
If I do that,
will you place your hand on the book
and promise?

'You don't have to,' said Merryn.

Hamish let out a long shaky breath. 'Yes I do,' he said. 'If anything horrible happens to you it'll be my fault, and I'll never forgive myself.'

He placed his hand on the book, and although he was shaking from head to toe, he managed to say the words. 'I promise to help Merryn with the Quest. I won't tell anyone about the horse or the crystals or the necklace or the magic.' He hesitated for a moment. 'But if I start to tell anyone, please don't let me.'

He dropped the book, dashed to the door and turned the handle. 'Thank goodness it opens,' he said, 'and don't tell me to shut it again, because I won't.' He threw himself back on the bed. 'I've said I'll help and I will. Only I can't stand being locked in. It freaks me out.'

Merryn picked up the book as the words vanished and new ones began to appear.

Merryn
You have already faced great danger.
I do not doubt your courage
or your wish to set me free,
but you too must promise to go on
until we reach our goal.
You must keep the strictest secrecy.
Try not to ask for help from anyone,
but if you must, conceal your reasons well
for there are eyes and ears that wish me ill.
Now you must swear upon the book.

Without hesitation Merryn placed her hand on the book. 'I swear that I'll continue to the end. If I need help I won't say why. And I swear I won't breathe a word about any of it to anyone.'

The writing disappeared and the book closed itself.

'What now?' Hamish asked. 'It can't stop there.'

'It can do anything it likes,' said Merryn, 'and there's nothing we can do about it. We just have to wait until it tells us what to do.'

Hamish got off the bed and paced up and down the bedroom. Several times a minute he stopped and stared at the book. 'I wish we'd never promised. What if it makes us do something really scary?'

Merryn was thinking a similar thought, but she wasn't going to admit it. 'We'll just have to do it. If we follow the rules and stick together we'll be OK. But look, it's starting to write again.'

She grabbed Hamish by the hand and pulled him down beside her. 'Let's read it together.'

QUEST TO FREE KESTER
FROM THE WITCH'S SPELL.

'He's called Kester,' said Merryn. 'The horse is called Kester.'

'Funny name for a horse,' said Hamish, 'but why does a horse have a book?'

Merryn shrugged. 'He's a magical horse,' she said. 'So I suppose he can have anything he wants.'

Before they could discuss the matter further, more writing appeared.

General Instructions
Concerning the Preparation for All Challenges.

'All challenges,' Hamish squealed. 'How many are there going to be?'

Merryn grew impatient. 'How would I know?'

The next sentence brought an answer, although it wasn't a very satisfactory one.

I cannot tell the number of challenges.
It depends on events beyond my control.

Now please pay attention
to the general instructions.

Merryn
You must wear the necklace at all times.
Only take it off when you place it on the
wooden horse's head.
Do not let anyone else wear it,
not even Hamish.
And put all three crystals back in the sporran.

'That's not fair.' Hamish tossed the yellow crystal onto the bed. He put his hands on his hips and scowled. 'I thought it was mine to keep.'

Hamish
The necklace and crystals
must stay with Merryn.
They will protect you
as long as you stay close to her.
You do not need to carry the crystal
and you do not need to wear the necklace.

'I might not need to,' he said, 'but I want to. I don't see why we can't take turns.' He stuck out his bottom lip and pushed in front of Merryn so that he could read the words first.

Merryn
The first task is for you alone.
It is the only time you must venture out
without the sporran.
When you see the nature of the task
you will understand
why this is important.

Where the stones are full of holes,
where the seeds are hard and dry,
you will find a Selkie's charm.

Hamish scowled as the book closed itself. 'What's that supposed to mean? And why is it telling you and not me? And what's a Selkie anyway?'

'I haven't a clue,' she said. 'You go and ask Aunt Aggie. No, don't. If it's something magical you'd better ask Donald. Don't tell him why we want to know. Just say we found the word in a book.'

As soon as Hamish had gone downstairs, she grabbed the key and let herself into the cubbyhole. She opened the box of sea-beans and hag-stones. There was nothing to catch her eye. She touched the sea-beans one by one but they all looked exactly the same.

'Show me,' she said, 'please.'

Her hand reached out and picked up a sea-bean. It looked like all the others, but when she looked more carefully she noticed a fine line running round the middle. It was as if some skilled craftsman had cut it in two and turned it into a box, a secret place for hiding something special.

Pushing her thumbnails into the join she started to prise the two halves apart. She'd only opened it a crack when the room was filled with a scent that made her nose wrinkle. It was the salty tang of the sea, heavy with seaweed, fish and the tarry smell of ropes. Before she had time to open it properly, she heard Hamish coming back upstairs.

'I know what a Selkie is,' he called. 'You're not going to believe this but it's a...' He stopped mid-sentence. 'Where are you, Merryn?'

Now that he'd promised to help, she felt mean keeping the cubbyhole to herself, but somehow she couldn't help it. She didn't answer his call, and after a moment's silence she heard him going downstairs.

Holding the Selkie's charm she slipped out of the cubbyhole and sat on the bed. She was just starting to open it when Hamish reappeared.

'Merryn, how did you do that? You weren't here a moment ago. I've been looking for you everywhere, and I found out what a Selkie is. It's a...'

'Hush,' she said. 'Listen. I can hear the sea.' She pulled the two halves of the sea- bean apart. Inside was a tiny shell. Coiled like a snail shell it was streaked with purple. And when she put it to her ear the sound grew louder. It was the roar of waves, the rumble of shingle and the singing of seals.

'Listen,' she said. 'There's a voice. It's calling my name.'

Hamish came closer. 'I can't even see it, never mind hear it,' he grumbled.

'That's because I have to do the next task by myself. I'm sorry, but there must be a reason why you can't help.'

She placed the shell in her palm. It gave out a soft luminescent glow as if it held the moon inside its coils. And although she wished that Hamish could see it, to him, it simply wasn't there.

'It's not fair,' he said. 'I made all those stupid promises and now it's leaving me out.' He stamped across the room, opened the door and scowled at her. 'Well, if I'm not wanted I'll find something else to do. You can find out about Selkies for yourself.'

Chapter 13

Merryn looked more closely at the sea-bean box. There were tiny scratches that looked as if they might be writing. She peered through Hamish's magnifying glass and her eyes widened in surprise.

FOR MERRYN MACQUEEN
FOREVER GRATEFUL
ROANE - 1881.

The sounds from the shell grew louder. She could hear curling waves, singing seals and the cries of gulls. And woven through them all, her name came in a continuous whisper.

'Merryn, Merryn, Merryn.'

Once it must have spoken to her great-great-great-great grandmother. Now it was calling to her. Kester's Book opened again and the invisible pen began to write.

Merryn
Take the shell and be on the shore
at twelve o'clock.
Go alone. Tell no-one where you are going.
Throw the shell into the sea
and Roane will come to you.
Ask him for the crystal pendulum for without it
you will be unable to complete the Quest.

The hairs on the back of her neck prickled. Roane! It couldn't be the Roane who'd given the sea-bean box to Merryn MacQueen. No-one who had been alive in

1881 could be alive now. It was impossible. There must be a different Roane, just as she was a different Merryn.

Whoever Roane was, he was a stranger. Times without number she'd been told not to speak to strangers. How could she meet one on a lonely beach in the thickest mist she'd ever seen? She checked her watch. It was almost half past eleven. She couldn't see out of the window. Finding her way to the beach would be impossible. Perhaps the book meant midnight. She would wait until nightfall and Kester could take her. Her decision made, she went to return the shell to its hiding place. But when she picked up the sea-bean box it refused to open.

The pages of Kester's Book turned, and more words appeared.

You may need the crystal pendulum tonight.
You must place your trust in Roane.
Leave the cottage now or you will be too late.
If you delay all may be lost.

Her hand reached up to clutch the necklace, and once again, Kester's desperate cry filled her head. He was still trapped inside the fencepost. She had to rescue him. She had to face Roane, whoever he was. The sporran opened itself and Kester's Book shrank and slipped itself inside. Obeying instructions, she hid the sporran under her pillow and left it behind.

She pulled on her fleece, wrapped the shell in a tissue and popped it into her pocket. She tiptoed downstairs and sneaked past the kitchen where Aunt Aggie was listening to the radio. Quickly she pulled on her wellingtons and slipped out into the mist. Which way should she go? After a few paces she stopped and looked back. There was nothing to see. The cottage had disappeared. Panic rose in her throat, threatening to choke her. She stretched out her arms and tried to sense the way ahead. She could feel nothing. She took a few tentative steps, stumbled, picked herself up and reached out again. At last her fingers found the cold metal of the gate. Terrified of losing her way, she clung to it. It had taken too long to reach the end of the garden. At this rate she wouldn't reach the sea by twelve o'clock.

'Merryn,' called the voice from the shell, 'Merryn.'

She fumbled in her pocket, and as she brought out the tissue, the shell dropped to the ground. Its moon-like glow shone through the mist. It guided her towards it, and in less than a second it was back in her hand. It sent out a narrow beam of light, stretching ahead, showing her the way to go. Time was running out. She no longer hesitated. Grasping the shell tightly, she held it out in front of her, and using its light as a guide, she ran. Twice she tripped on the uneven ground. Twice she dropped the shell, but each time she found it and ran on. Eventually the track gave way to grass, and soon the grass gave way to the shore.

As her feet sank into the sand she stopped and listened to the murmur of waves. Right to the sea's edge she went, and when small waves began to break over her feet she stopped, raised her hand and prepared to throw the shell.

A whisper reached her ears. 'Not yet. Not yet. You must wait for the circle.'

She lowered her hand and frowned at the path of light that cut through the waves. There was no circle, just a straight line leading farther and farther into the sea. She turned to run back to safety, but before she'd taken a single step, Kester's frantic neighing filled her head, reminding her of what she had to do.

Hesitantly she stepped forwards, four paces, six paces. Still there was no sign of a circle. Ten paces, fifteen paces, and suddenly it appeared before her. A circle that was round as a full moon and twice as bright. But it was still way ahead and the sea was getting deeper. It poured over the top of her wellingtons and soaked into her socks. Still the light drew her on. Still the water rose. When it reached the top of her legs she began to sob.

The circle of light was still out of reach. She forced herself onwards until the sea rose up to her waist. Then, almost paralysed with fear, she stopped. It was impossible. She looked back to where the shore must be, but there was no sign of it. The path of light along which she'd come had disappeared. She was stranded, freezing cold, lost among waves that broke against her body and splashed her face.

'Mum, Dad,' she screamed. 'Help me.'

But her parents were far away. They knew nothing of the danger she was in. No-one knew where she was, not Aunt Aggie, not even Hamish. Roane! If he really was coming to meet her, he must know where she was.

'Roane,' she sobbed, 'Please help me.'

'Two more steps,' the voice replied.

She was no longer alone. Her courage returned. Two steps brought her to the edge of the circle of light.

The voice spoke again. 'Now Merryn, throw it now.'

Relief flooded through her as she lifted the shell high above her head and hurled it. It curved in an arc, hit the sea's surface and sent lilac ripples spreading throughout the circle. She turned and tried to hurry back, but a sudden surge caught her. It knocked her over, dragged her under and threatened to sweep her into deeper water. Coughing and spluttering she struggled to her feet. The light that marked the pathway from the circle to the shore had re-appeared, but it seemed fainter than before.

Weeping with anxiety she battled along it, though it was not until the water level dropped to her knees that she began to breathe more easily. She broke into a run, splashed her way through the shallows and collapsed on the sand. Pulling off her wellingtons, she tipped out a stream of seawater. She squeezed the water out of her socks and pushed them into her pocket. Then, forcing her bare feet back into her wellingtons, she sat shivering with cold, hoping desperately that Roane would not keep her waiting.

The mist seemed thicker than ever. It pressed in on her, threatening to smother her. She held her hand in front of her face, but even with it touching her nose, she couldn't see a single finger. She closed her eyes and listened. Above the murmur of the sea she heard the beat of her heart. It thudded so insistently that she could bear it no longer.

'Roane,' she screamed. 'Please hurry.'

'Merryn,' her name came whispering through the mist.

It was a soothing sound that stilled her heart and made her raise her head. A strange eerie glow had formed. It moved towards her, closer and closer, growing as it came. It was not a pathway like the light from the shell. It was not a circle like the light in the sea. It was a light in the shape of a man, a man leaning on a stick, limping as if he was either very old or very tired.

She knew at once that he was no mortal man. But if he was not a man, what was he? The word that was in Kester's Book had slipped her mind. She'd sent Hamish to find its meaning, only she hadn't given him the chance to tell her. Now she was going to find out.

She stared at the silvery-blue ripple of the man's hair. It hung in tendrils round his face. It merged with a beard of the same colour. It lay on the shoulders of a fur cape of mottled grey. Sudden fear took hold of her. Her hands and feet pushed and scrabbled at the damp sand as she tried to back away from him.

Chapter 14

'Merryn, Merryn,' said the man as he came closer. 'Surely you are not afraid of me, not after all that has passed between us. Truly it is many a long year since last we met. Even so I had not expected this. Perhaps it was the sea that scared you. I am sorry that you had to venture into such deep water, but I could not retrieve the shell in the shallows.'

He took off his cape and wrapped it gently round her shaking shoulders. Gratefully, she huddled into it, and her teeth gradually stopped chattering as its warmth began to penetrate her wet clothes.

'You called me and I came,' he said. 'Surely you can look at me.'

She recognised his voice. It was the voice from the shell. It carried with it the sound of the sea. It was a medley of sea breezes, rippling waves and songs of seals. There was kindness in it too, and the necklace of sea-beans and hag-stones began to tingle as if to tell her that she could trust him. She looked into his face and saw that his eyes were like pools of the sea, silvery blue and deep as the ocean. And when he grasped her hands, she did not pull away.

'You are Merryn,' he said in a puzzled tone. 'Yet you are not my Merryn. Why have you come in her place? Where is she? And why do you have need of me?'

Filled with confusion she looked away. Could he really have known that other Merryn of long ago? If this island world was filled with enchanted horses and evil witches, it must be possible for strange men to live for a hundred years. She felt a wave of sadness as she wondered how to tell him that Merryn was no longer alive.

He let go of her hands and placed his palms together. 'Ah! I understand your silence. I had forgotten that mortal lifespan is short. My Merryn has passed away and your world is the worse for having lost her.'

His eyes overflowed with tears. 'She was the wisest, kindest mortal of them all. Were it not for her, I too would have died long ago. My bones would have crumbled to dust in yonder graveyard. Come, sit with me and we will talk, for I have questions needing answers.'

Once more he took her by the hand and led her to the dune edge. There, he sat down and stretched out his lame leg. 'Tell me,' he said, 'How did you find the shell, and what do you want of me?'

'The trouble is,' Merryn began. 'I don't understand any of it. It all started when I heard a horse calling for help. Then I found this.' She unzipped her fleece and showed him the necklace of sea-beans and hag-stones.

He reached out to touch it and although his face broke into a smile, his eyes brimmed with sadness. 'I have one too.' He moved his collar aside to show her a necklace that was identical to hers. 'Merryn and I made them together. When my people learned of all that she had done for me, they felt it their duty to protect her. They collected the sea-beans and hag-stones and sent them on the tide to this very shore.'

'What had she done for you?' Merryn asked. 'And why did she need protecting?'

'I will tell you before I leave. However, you must first answer my questions. You are in danger and you have asked for help, otherwise the shell would not have called me. So tell me why you are here.'

'There's a witch,' Merryn explained. 'She trapped a horse inside a fence post and when I used the necklace to set him free, she swore she'd kill me. The trouble is, the necklace didn't break the spell completely. He went back into the post at sunrise and I'm trying to free him for ever. I found a book that tells me what to do. It told me to come to you.'

Roane touched his finger to her lips. 'There is no need to tell me more,' he said. 'Kester has been captive for many years. If my Merryn had been alive she would have done as you are doing. She too would have risked all to save him. For she, like you, had The Gift. But it has led you into great danger and I fear for your safety. In your world, much of the benevolent magic has been lost, malevolence is growing, and there are few left who can help in your Quest to free the world from evil.'

'That's not what I'm doing,' Merryn protested. 'I'm just freeing Kester from the witch's spell.'

'That may have been your intention,' he said, 'but there is far more at stake. The witch will pursue you even if you abandon the horse. You have freed him once and she is afraid that you will free him again. She will do all in her power to stop you and she will fight to her last breath. She has sworn to kill the horse and she will put an end to anyone who stands in her way.'

Despite the warmth of the sealskin, Merryn began to shiver. Whether she carried on or turned away, the danger would always be there. The cloak no longer warmed her. Drops of icy water fell from her hair and trickled down her neck. Thoughts of what the witch might do filled her with a fear that seemed to freeze her very bones.

'But why does the witch want to kill him?' she asked.

'I believe it is a matter of honour. I understand that the Malevolent Witches banished her. If she kills Kester she will be allowed to return. It is part of a great battle between good and evil, and I fear that you have been drawn into it. I am sorry that you did not realise the enormity of your undertaking. It is a heavy burden to bear, but The Gift let you hear Kester's cry for help, and once you heard it, you could not forget it.'

'If I'd known all this I wouldn't have listened. I would have buried my head under my pillow. I would never...'

Terrified neighing broke into her words. She stopped, pulled off the necklace and dropped it on the sand. She clapped her hands over her ears, but even without the necklace, the desperate cry went on and on and on. She was trapped between fear of the witch and Kester's insistent plea for help.

'I can't go back on my word,' she sobbed. 'He won't let me. He's inside my head and he won't let me go.'

Very gently, Roane slipped the necklace back over her head and wrapped the cloak more tightly round her shoulders.

'It's The Gift that lets you hear him,' he said. 'Until he is rescued, you will hear him whether or not you wear the necklace. And if you want him to stop calling, you must reassure him. Let him know that you will hold to your promise.'

'I will,' she cried. 'I promise. I'll do all I can to help. I want to save you, I really do, just get out of my head. Please.'

The cries faded into silence. She slumped against Roane and he put his arm around her shoulders.

'If anyone can succeed,' he said. 'You can, but you must wear the necklace at all times for it will deter the witch. However, I must warn you that she will make even stronger magic, and I cannot tell how long the necklace will hold out against her. For that reason you must make haste. The sooner you end the Quest, the less time she will have to develop new spells. Each night that passes must take you a step nearer to your goal. You need something from me to help you on your way. I think I know what it is, but I must hear it from your own lips.'

'I was told to ask for the crystal pendulum. I don't know what I have to do with it. I don't even know what it is, and I don't like asking for things when I have nothing to give in return.'

Roane smiled. 'Meeting you has been reward enough. I need nothing and I expect nothing. Providing that the crystal pendulum responds to you, I will gladly give it into your keeping.'

Chapter 15

Merryn watched anxiously as Roane reached inside his shirt and pulled out a chain of gold. Dangling from the end of it was a crystal. It sparkled with all the colours of the rainbow. It shimmered with colours that came from beyond rainbows. It brought a gasp from her lips, but would it respond to her?

Roane suspended the crystal over her open palm, Warmth radiated from it. The chill that had enveloped her began to diminish. Slowly the pendulum began to sway. She laughed in delight as it settled into a rhythm, moving smoothly in a figure of eight. Over and over again, it drew the pattern that has no beginning and no end.

Roane smiled and gave a satisfied nod. 'It is as I thought. You see it clearly, and it responds to you. I do not fully understand its power, but I know that mortals who have The Gift can see it, and other mortals cannot. I know too, that magical beings can only see it if their purpose is honest and true.'

He slipped the chain over her head and tucked the pendulum inside her fleece. 'Keep it hidden,' he said, 'or it will dazzle your eyes. If you have doubts about who to trust, lift it out. If they see it, all will be well. If they do not see it, you must be on your guard.'

'And must I wear it all the time?' she asked.

'Indeed you must, for that is the only way to keep it safe. If you need to use it, the chain will lengthen, so you do not need to take it off. At times of greatest need, suspend it from your finger, and it may be able to help you. I do not know if it can foil the witch's spells because I have never put it to the test. That is something you will have to discover for yourself.'

Merryn rested her chin on her cupped hand. 'Well, it must be able to do something,' she said, 'otherwise I wouldn't have been told to get it.'

'It may be that your task is simply to return it to the one who lost it. It is not yours and never can be. When the time comes you must give it up gladly, for without it, I believe its true owner is lost between worlds.'

Merryn looked at Roane with puzzled eyes. 'This gets harder and harder to understand,' she said. 'I thought it belonged to you. Why were you wearing it if it isn't yours? And who is its true owner?'

'I wear it because I found it on the sea bed many moons ago, and I have kept it safe until it is needed. That time has come and although there will be obstacles in its path, it is starting a journey back to its true owner. Guard it well, and when you complete the Quest you will discover who that is for yourself.'

The first challenge was over, but it had brought more questions than answers. Deep in thought Merryn stared into mist that was as thick as ever. Yet, she was sitting in a pool of sea-green light that shone from a Selkie. A Selkie named Roane who had known the Merryn MacQueen of long ago. Hamish would never believe her.

'Hamish!' she exclaimed. 'I don't mind for myself, but what about my brother? I'm supposed to be looking after him, and all I've done is lead him into danger.' A feeling of despair washed over her. 'Why have I got The Gift? And why is it called a gift when it feels like a curse.' She looked up at Roane. 'I can't risk my brother's life,' she sobbed. 'Please help me. Please take The Gift away.'

Roane shook his head. 'I am sorry but I cannot. The Gift arrived at your birth and it will be with you until the end of your days. I understand your fear, for it is a mixed blessing. Somehow, you must learn to live with it. Like my Merryn, you must find ways of using it to help your fellow mortals.'

'But how can I do that? Help me to understand,' she begged. 'Tell me how Merryn did it. Tell me what happened all those years ago'.

'Ah!' Roane said. 'I cannot tell you what to do but I will tell you of my Merryn. It all began with a girl called Catriona. She had hair as black as a raven's wing and eyes as blue as forget-me-nots. Her singing was so beautiful that it drew me out of the sea to listen.'

'Out of the sea!' exclaimed Merryn. 'Whatever do you mean?'

'I mean that my true home is in the sea for I am a Selkie. Surely you knew that the shell was a Selkie's charm.'

'Yes, the book told me, only it didn't tell me what a Selkie was, and I still don't know.'

'A Selkie is a seal that can leave the sea, take off its sealskin and take on the guise of a human.' He stretched out his fingers to show her the webbing between. 'This is one part of me that cannot change, even when I take the form of a man.'

Merryn looked at his hand in bewilderment.

'I know,' he said. 'It is hard to believe, and there is more. If a Selkie accepts your human lifespan it can live in your world. I was prepared to do that for Catriona. I told her of my love and for proof she asked for treasures from the sea. She wanted things that lay in the holds of sunken ships. I brought her goblets and coins of gold. I brought her jewels and plates of the finest china. When she tired of those she asked for the most perfect pearls. I brought them to her one by one, day after day. She would not let me stop until her casket was full.'

A frown grew on Merryn's face as she listened. 'That was greedy,' she exclaimed. 'You should have refused.'

'I know that now,' he agreed, 'for one casket was not enough. She found another and said that if I truly loved her I would fill that one too. By that time I was weary of seeking for pearls. I was sorry too, for the oysters I had plundered. So I showed her the necklace that had belonged to my mother and to all the mothers who came before her. It was made of one hundred perfect pearls. It was the most beautiful necklace that ever came out of the sea.'

Merryn couldn't stop herself from interrupting. 'And I suppose she wanted that too. I hope you didn't give it to her.'

'You show great wisdom,' he said. 'You can see where my folly was leading. But no, I did not give it to her. I told her that it would be hers on the day she married me.'

'But I don't understand. Why did you want to marry her when she was so horribly greedy?'

'Why indeed? I was powerless because she had bewitched me. She had dazzled me with her beauty and enchanted me with her singing. She promised to be my wife, but she would not wait for the necklace. She snatched it from me and fastened it round her neck. I should have known that there was neither love nor kindness in her heart. But her power came from knowledge of malevolent magic. It blinded my eyes and befuddled my brain. Besides, she had possession of the necklace that was destined for my wife. Without it I could not marry, for the necklace that has been handed down through generations is an essential part of a Selkie's marriage pledge. So you see, I had to marry her or spend the rest of my days alone.'

'You should have taken it back,' protested Merryn. 'She didn't deserve to keep it.'

Roane gave a rueful smile. 'Wise child,' he said. 'I pray that love for the wrong person never blinds your eyes as it blinded mine. I tried to take it from her, but she would not let go. Between us we snapped the string. The pearls scattered across the sand. I fell to my knees and counted them. As long as I could find them all, the necklace could be mended. But three were missing. That's when I realised that Catriona was missing too. I forgot the pearls for a sudden fear came into my heart. She knew where I kept my sealskin. I ran as fast as I could, but when I reached the hiding place, my sealskin had gone.'

Chapter 16

'Catriona stole my sealskin out of spite,' said Roane. 'All I wanted was to return to the sea, but without my sealskin I was stranded on dry land. I searched everywhere, and when I eventually found Catriona, another girl was with her.'

Pausing for a moment, he touched Merryn's hair. 'You have inherited her colouring, for her hair, like yours was the colour of bracken in autumn. Her eyes too, were flecked with gold.'

'It was Merryn,' she whispered. 'It was Merryn, wasn't it?'

Roane nodded. 'She tried to take my sealskin from Catriona, but Catriona would not let go. As she pulled and tugged, my body was wrenched this way and that. It was agony. I could barely stand, and before I could reach them I saw the flash of a knife. Catriona slashed the skin and I fell to the ground with blood pouring from my leg.'

'No!' Merryn cried out. It was too awful to believe. She wanted to ask what happened next, but Roane seemed weary. He gave a long sigh and stared into the mist. He rubbed his injured leg as if speaking of it had re-awakened the pain.

'And you still limp because of the cut from Catriona's knife,' she said.

'That is so. Only that was not the end of it. Catriona swore that it was Merryn who had stolen my sealskin. I knew that was not true and I told her that I no longer wished to marry her. In the days that followed she vented all her anger on Merryn, and she used witchcraft to help her. That is why my people collected the sea-beans and hag-stones. And that is why I helped Merryn to thread them into a necklace. As soon as Catriona saw it she knew she had lost, and she left the island taking all her treasures with her.'

'Not the three pearls,' said Merryn. 'Don't tell me she took the three pearls.'

'No, she did not,' said Roane with a smile. 'Merryn found them for me. But before that she tore a strip from her petticoat and bound my leg to stop the bleeding. Then she ran home to fetch her husband. They took me to their cottage and she tended my wound until I was able to walk again. She sewed my sealskin with the finest thread and the greatest care. Her work was meticulous and the repair has served me well. When I am in the sea, it hardly hinders me at all. Now that I am back on land it pains me and makes me limp.'

'I'm sorry,' said Merryn as she laid her hand on his knee. 'It's my fault for calling you out of the sea. I'm so very sorry.'

'Do not apologise,' he said. 'I am glad that you called me. It is good to know that there is still a Merryn in possession of The Gift. But let me finish my story. While I waited for my wound to heal I carved a wee box out of a sea-bean.'

Merryn's face lit up. 'I found it,' she said, 'and the shell was inside.'

'That's because I put it there,' he said. 'I told my Merryn to throw it into the sea if she ever needed me. I waited and waited. I longed to see her again but the call never came. Until today I did not venture out of the sea again. Now I must give the shell back to you.'

He reached into his pocket, pulled it out and placed it in her hand. 'Put it back in the sea-bean box, and guard it well, for one day, you may need it again.'

Merryn shook her head in wonder as she looked at the shell. It was such a tiny thing. Yet it had shown her a world that lay far beyond her thoughts and dreams. It had shown her Roane. She smiled up into his eyes.

'Thank you,' she said. 'I'll treasure it for ever.'

'You are truly welcome,' he said. 'Thanks to my Merryn, the pearl necklace was repaired. I married a Selkie and I have fine sons who will answer the call of the shell if I am gone.'

He struggled to his feet, lifted the sealskin cloak from her shoulders and placed it around his own. 'As for the time that has passed between us, no-one will ever know. I brought you out of mortal time. All that we have shared took no more than a moment. When you are back in your own time you will be as dry as you were before you went into the sea. So go now. Make ready for the next part of your Quest. Be brave and face whatever lies ahead. My good wishes go with you.'

With that he turned and limped into the mist. A great wave of sadness washed over her for she sensed that she would never see him again. He had told her many things about the first Merryn MacQueen. Now she was desperate to know more. She opened her mouth to call him back, but the glow from his body was fading into the distance, and a second later he had disappeared.

She felt as if she'd been with him for hours, yet when she looked at her watch by the light from the seashell, she saw that his words were true. Time had hardly passed at all. She would be able to get back before Aunt Aggie missed her.

The mist had not thinned at all but the light from the shell showed her the way. With five minutes to spare she was back inside her bedroom. She sat on the bed and pulled the crystal pendulum from inside her fleece. The light that shone from it was far greater than the light from the three small crystals. She twisted it backwards and forwards in her hand. The beams from it cast dancing rainbows all over the walls and ceiling. It was wonderful, incredible, spectacular, but even as she watched, doubts began to flood her mind.

Roane's story about Merryn had been amazing, but it had distracted her. For a short while it had taken her mind away from the Quest. It had made her forget the terrifying walk into the sea. Now she remembered the danger she'd been in, and she thought of the dangers still to come. Tonight she must release the horse from the fence post. Tonight she would have another task to perform. Tonight she would face the witch again, and the witch would try to stop her.

Chapter 17

Lunchtime was an ordeal. Hamish scowled at Merryn throughout the meal. He ate in silence, cleared the table, washed the dishes and went straight back to his room.

'What's the matter with him?' Aunt Aggie asked. 'Have you two been falling out?'

Merryn shrugged as if she hadn't a clue why Hamish was in such a bad mood. 'I think he's fed up because he can't go down to the shore,' she said.

It wasn't true. She knew exactly what was wrong, but she couldn't tell Aunt Aggie. She couldn't say that he was sulking because he'd been left out of the first task. Or that he was angry because he wasn't allowed to wear the necklace of sea-beans and hag-stones.

Well, she thought, he ought to think himself lucky. He hadn't been forced to walk into the sea. If he'd done that he would have been out of his depth. He might even have drowned, and she would have been to blame.

She went back to her room and grabbed the sporran. It wouldn't open. Her voice rose in anger. 'You knew I had to go into the sea. You made me leave the sporran behind because you didn't want it to get wet.'

The sporran opened, the book leapt out and words appeared in reply.

> *Yes, I knew but I had faith in you*
> *and we will not reach our goal*
> *without the crystal pendulum.*

'It's not our goal,' she snapped. 'It's your goal. I promised to help and I will, but I won't let you send Hamish into danger. You've got to let him back out.'

That I cannot do.
Only he can ask to be released from his promise.

Merryn retorted angrily, 'Then I'll make him ask.'

I do not think you will be able to do that.

'Well, I'll jolly well try.' She left the book on the bed, marched out of the room and knocked on Hamish's door.

'Go away,' he yelled.

'No, I won't'. She opened the door. 'I've done my task. I had to wade into the sea and...'

'Don't talk rubbish,' he said. 'You haven't been anywhere. There wasn't time to get to the shore and back.' He clamped his hands over his ears and turned his back.

Merryn pulled his hands away and held them tight while she forced him to listen. 'It's true. I met the Selkie and he gave me the crystal pendulum. I'm glad you didn't come because it was dangerous. You've got to ask Kester's Book to let you back out.'

'I will not.' Hamish wrenched his hands away. 'You just want to keep everything to yourself. I made a promise and I'm going to keep it.'

'And I promised Dad that I'd try and keep you out of trouble.'

'Well you tried and you failed,' Hamish retorted, 'and you're not my keeper. So stop bossing me about. I'm not staying behind while you have all the fun.'

'Fun,' she exclaimed. 'It was terrifying. I had to walk into the sea. I could have drowned. You're not helping and that's that.'

'You can't stop me.' He grabbed her arm as she turned to leave.

She tried to shake him off, but he wouldn't let go. He hung on until they were inside her bedroom. Then he pushed her away and glared.

Merryn glared back. 'If the book says you can't help, you can't help so there's no point in sulking.'

'I'll sulk as much as I like,' he said, 'and if it leaves me out again I'll sulk even more.'

Before Merryn could reply, a new message began to appear.

Merryn and Hamish

As soon as he saw his name, Hamish grinned. He punched her arm. 'See,' he said. 'I have to help.'

Merryn's heart sank. She couldn't stop him, but that wouldn't stop her from worrying. 'OK. You win,' she said. 'Only you must do exactly as the book says. I don't want you to get hurt.'

'I won't,' he said. 'I promise I'll be careful. I don't even care if it's dangerous. It's exciting.' He squeezed her hand. 'Come on, let's read what we have to do. Whatever it is, we'll do it together.'

Tonight you will both ride Kester.

'Yippee!' Hamish cheered. 'I'm going to ride him.'

Take the silver bell.

'We haven't got a silver bell,' he said.

'Not just any bell,' said Merryn. 'It says 'the silver bell'. It must be a special one. Maybe it's in the sporran.'

The sporran opened, she slipped her hand inside, and with a satisfied nod drew out an elaborately engraved silver bell. She was just about to ring it when more words appeared.

Put the silver bell back in the sporran.
It will not ring until you take it
to Fang an t-Sithein.

'Where on earth's that?' Hamish asked.

'I've no idea. We'll ask Donald,' said Merryn, 'but we mustn't tell him why we want to know.'

Kester will take you to
Fang an t-Sithein tonight.
Do not try to find it for yourselves.
The Fairy Folk will not be pleased
if you go during the day.

'Fairies!' exclaimed Hamish. 'I don't believe in fairies.'

The book snapped shut on Hamish's fingers. He winced and took a step back.

'You shouldn't have said that,' said Merryn. 'You believe in the crystals. You'll believe in the witch when you see her. So you'd better believe in fairies too.'

Hamish laughed nervously. The speed of the book's response had shocked him and the slap to his fingers had really hurt. 'I'm sorry,' he mumbled. 'It's just that fairies are girly stuff.'

The book was still closed. Merryn drummed her fingers impatiently while she waited for it to open. 'If you've spoiled everything I'll never forgive you. You have to believe. You have to trust the book. If you don't there's no point to any of it.'

Two minutes passed. She was just about to plead with the book to continue the instructions, when more writing appeared.

Hamish
Do not doubt the existence of fairies.
Keep an open mind at all times.
In the world of magic anything is possible.
Tonight you will meet the witch.
She will try everything in her power
to stop you.
Stay close to Merryn
and do not let the witch see that you are afraid.
She feeds on the fear of her adversaries
and by that means her power will grow.

What's an adversary?' Hamish asked.

'I think it means us, enemies, people who are challenging her,' Merryn replied.

You will meet the Fairy Folk too.
Be aware that you cannot be too careful
where fairies are concerned.
Do not try to deceive them.
Speak always with absolute honesty.

Hamish
You will keep hold of Kester.

Merryn
I will give you words to learn
because you will do the talking.
Tonight you must take the silver bell
to Fang an t-Sithein
and you must ask the Fairy Folk
to exchange it for the heart-stone.

'What's a heart-stone,' asked Hamish.

'How would I know? We'll have to wait and see,' said Merryn. 'Now be quiet while I learn the words.'

She read the sentences over and over. She practiced until she knew them by heart. Eventually, as if it was satisfied, the book closed. It shrank and slipped itself into the sporran. It obviously had nothing more to tell.

For hours, the witch had ridden round the island. She had enough birch twigs for the end of the broom, but she hadn't found a suitable shaft. The only ash tree she'd seen was growing in the churchyard, and when she'd tried to pass through the gate, the consecrated ground had forced her back. As a last resort she'd broken a branch from the only tree that grows to any height on the windswept island.

'Ake-ake,' she murmured. 'The name itself has a magic ring to it, but will it fly? It has to fly. It's my only chance.'

As she reached the souterrain, she raised her hands and dispelled the mist. Once inside, she tossed the willow bark, the birch twigs and the Ake-ake branch into a corner. Far too exhausted to make the new broom immediately, she lay down and slept.

'Hey, the mist's gone.' Hamish grabbed his fleece. 'I'm going to the shore. See you later.'

Merryn watched him racing down the track. It would be fun to join him, but her thoughts were on Fang an t-Sithein. Kester's book had told her not to go in search of it, but surely there would be no harm in finding out what the name meant. Donald was bound to know so she ran across to his cottage to ask.

He greeted her with a smile. 'What is it this time? More Gaelic?'

Merryn nodded. 'What does Fang mean?' she asked.

'It's Gaelic for a fank, an enclosure where they gather the sheep for dipping and shearing.'

'And sithein,' she spelled it out, 's i t h e i n - what's that?'

'You mean 'shee-hen'. It's a fairy mound. Why do you want to know?'

'It's mentioned in a book,' said Merryn. 'I thought it sounded interesting. So what does Fang an t-Sithein mean?

'I suppose it means the enclosure of the fairies. It sounds like a little green hill with a wall round it.' He shook his head. 'I can't think of anything like that on Tiree. There are fairy mounds though.'

'Do you believe in fairies?' she asked.

'Maybe I do,' he said. 'I was brought up on tales of them stealing babies. I guess that's made me wary of saying anything against them.'

Merryn gasped. She'd hoped that the Fairy Folk would be kind and helpful like Roane. Now, her confidence wavered. Was meeting them going to be dangerous? She had to know. 'Is it just babies, or do they steal other things?' she asked.

'They lure people into their mounds,' he said, 'and they keep them captive for a night. Only it isn't a mortal night. When they're set free they find that years have gone by, everyone they knew has died and they suddenly grow old.'

A wave of nausea washed over Merryn. She swayed unsteadily, grabbed the chair and sat down.

Donald laughed. 'Don't look so worried,' he said. 'I don't suppose it's true, although my granny used to say that you can't be too careful where fairies are concerned.'

'That's what...' Merryn closed her lips and turned away. She'd heard those words before. She'd been warned about the danger of associating with fairies. And tonight she had to go and meet them.

Chapter 18

'Off to the tent now,' said Aunt Aggie when supper was over. 'I'm ready for bed and I don't want disturbing.'

Neither Hamish nor Merryn needed to be told a second time. They were both tired. Hamish had spent a long time clambering among rock pools. And in addition to her ordeal in the sea, Merryn had slept little on the previous night. Knowing they needed to rest before the night's adventure, they went out to the tent without a word of complaint.

Down in the souterrain the witch awoke with a start. It was twenty past ten. She cursed herself for leaving so little time to make the new broomstick. She gathered the birch twigs together and tried to bind them to the Ake-ake branch. She wrapped the cord as tightly as she could, but when she let go it came loose. She muttered spells under her breath. She shouted spells out loud. Nothing worked. No matter what she said or did, the twigs kept falling to the floor.

'Curses,' she fumed. 'I need ash. That's why it won't work.'

In disgust she threw the Ake-ake branch to one side. The only ash available was the shaft of the broken broomstick. She inspected it closely. The split in the handle started at one end, but it hadn't reached the other

'I wonder,' she said, 'if new twigs on the old shaft will work.'

She glanced at her watch. 'Nearly eleven,' she moaned. 'I must go soon. I can't let that wretched girl release Kester again.'

Hurriedly she stripped off the old birch twigs and attached the new ones as tightly as she could. Then she wound the rest of the cord round and round the shaft as far as it would go. She went to the souterrain entrance, looked out into the night, mounted the broomstick and ordered it to fly. It had barely risen from the ground when it wobbled and made a crash landing..

'Curse you,' she shrieked as she climbed aboard again. 'Fly. Curse you, fly.'

The broomstick tried to rise. It quivered and lay still. With another curse she carried it back into the souterrain. There on the floor, half-hidden by the discarded birch twigs, lay the strips of willow bark.

'Stupid,' she said. 'How could I have been so stupid? Of course the cord won't hold. It has to be willow bark.'

She wound the strips round the damaged shaft and this time they did not unravel. She brought the shaft close to her nose and peered at it through half-closed eyes. The split was barely visible. She mounted and willed the broomstick to fly. It rose into the air and gathered speed. With a satisfied nod she checked the time. It was half past eleven.

'Should I go to the cottage and stop the girl from leaving?' she asked herself. 'Or should I go straight to the post?'

As she swung away from the souterrain she made her decision.

It was also eleven thirty when Merryn's alarm sounded. To her surprise Hamish was out of his sleeping bag before she'd stopped the persistent beeping.

'Come on,' he said. 'I can't wait to ride Kester. He dressed quickly and started to open the tent flap. 'Let's go.'

Merryn grabbed his arm and pulled him back. 'We go out together,' she said. 'You've got to stay close to me otherwise ...'

'Otherwise what?' he demanded.

'I don't know,' said Merryn. 'It's what Kester's Book told you to do. If you go out by yourself the witch might...'

'Might what?'

'She might do something horrible. If you stay with me you'll have some protection from the necklace and the crystals. At least that's what the book said. So I'm going first and you can follow.'

'I don't see why I always have to be last,' he grumbled.

Merryn ignored him. She stepped out of the tent into the moonlight, and pointed towards the gate.

'That's why,' she said.

Hamish peered round her shoulder. 'Oh! crumbs,' he squealed. 'I can see her. I can see the witch.' His voice rose in panic. 'She's going to stop us. She's...'

Merryn pushed him back into the tent and shook him by the shoulders. 'Stop it,' she said. 'You've got to be brave.'

Grabbing him by the hand she pulled him out of the tent, and although her heart felt as if it was thumping in her throat, she marched determinedly up the path.

The witch stood by the gate with the broomstick in her hand. 'Go back,' she snarled. 'Don't interfere with things that don't concern you.'

Merryn kept on walking.

The witch's snarl turned to a scream. 'Go back. Go back.'

Merryn didn't falter. Dragging Hamish along with her she walked straight towards the witch. The witch held up her hands as if to protect herself. She was being forced backwards, one step, two steps, three.

'See,' whispered Merryn. 'She can't get near us. When I count three run as fast as you can. Run straight at her. One, two...'

Before Merryn finished counting the witch had climbed onto her broomstick and was heading in the direction of the wooden post. Still grasping Hamish by the hand, Merryn ran after her.

'I saw a bubble,' said Hamish. 'It's true. She can't touch us. We're inside a bubble. Did you see it, Merryn?'

'Shh! We haven't time to talk,' she said. 'We've got to release Kester before the witch tries another spell. Save your breath for running.'

'But I saw it,' he insisted. 'It's a giant bubble and it pushed her away.'

'Let's hope you're right,' Merryn panted. 'Now stop talking and run.'

A few minutes later, out of breath and anxious, they arrived at the field. The post was still there, but so was the witch. She was standing by a heap of old fence posts and she was whirling one of them above her head.

'Come any closer,' she said, 'and I'll burst your beastly bubble.'

'See,' said Hamish. 'I was right. She knows we're in a bubble and she's going to burst it.'

'She'll try,' said Merryn. 'But we've got to believe that she can't. We've got to hope she's bluffing. Remember what the book said. Our fear makes her stronger. Keep behind me and don't let her see that you're scared.'

With Hamish holding onto the back of her fleece, Merryn went into the field. The witch tried again to block their way. She threw the fencepost towards them. It flew over their heads, bounced off the top of the bubble and landed with a thud behind them. Merryn couldn't help ducking, and as she did so, Hamish slipped and let out a scream.

The witch roared with laughter. 'What's that behind you? A wee wimp of a boy! He's not going to help you. He's so scared he can't even stand up.'

Hamish struggled to his knees, but before he could stand, the witch hurled another fencepost. It came so close that it hit the bubble and showered it with a stream of sparks. Merryn flinched but managed not to duck. Hamish buried his head in his hands and stifled a sob.

'Get up,' Merryn hissed. She grabbed him by the collar and hauled him to his feet. 'Show her you're not a wimp. And if you are a wimp just pretend that you're not.'

'He is a wimp,' the witch shouted. 'Look at him. His knees are knocking. His teeth are chattering.'

Hamish knocked Merryn's hand away and mumbled under his breath. 'I'm not a wimp.'

'Then pull yourself together and tell her,' said Merryn. 'Go on, prove it.'

'My knees aren't knocking,' he shouted. 'My teeth aren't chattering and I'm not a wimp.'

'Good for you,' said Merryn. 'Now prove it.'

As Merryn pulled him along, the witch flew to the post and folded her arms around it. Hamish tried to pull Merryn back, but she yanked his arm and kept on walking. The witch held onto the post as long as she could, but the bubble was forcing her away. Her feet left the ground, her body floated in the air, but her arms were still wrapped round the post.

'We'll have to take her by surprise,' whispered Merryn. 'Take three steps back, then when I squeeze your hand we'll rush forwards together.'

As they retreated, the witch's feet dropped back to the ground. She gave a triumphant screech. 'You're both wimps,' she shouted. 'You've given up already. Go on, run away. You're no match for me.'

Merryn squeezed Hamish's hand and they charged. Taken unawares, the witch lost her grip and was thrown over backwards.

'I'll get you for this,' she snarled as she picked herself up. 'You may have won this day but there are other days to come. I'll watch your every move. I'll find out how your magic works. I'll make new spells. I'll get the better of you if it's the last thing I do.'

Chapter 19

The witch spat like a bad-tempered cat. She pressed her face against the bubble and bared her teeth. Merryn, trying desperately to ignore her, turned her back and rested her cheek against the post. She took off the necklace and slipped it over the wooden horse's head. There was a flash of silver light and the necklace lengthened. Once again the fence post was wreathed in bright colours and surrounded by sweet music. For a few magical moments Hamish seemed to forget the witch. He swivelled round and round, staring in surprise at the swirl of rainbow threads.

Merryn grew impatient. 'Hurry, please hurry,' she said. 'The witch is here and there's no time to lose.'

The threads twirled more wildly and as the music rose to a crescendo Kester appeared beside them. Merryn flung her arms round his neck and Hamish squealed with delight. But their smiles vanished as the witch began to prance around the bubble. She waved her broomstick and chanted a string of strange words. Kester stamped his feet and gave a terrified neigh.

'Quick, we've got to leave before she finishes her spell.' Merryn leapt onto Kester's back and pulled Hamish up behind her. As softly as she could, she whispered, 'to Fang an t-Sithein.'

The witch was still chanting as they left the field. Soon they'd crossed The Reef and were galloping along the wide expanse of Gott Bay. When they turned inland there was still no sign of the witch. Kester slowed to a canter, crossed a sloping field, stepped over a stretch of boggy ground and stopped. There in front of them lay a small grassy hill surrounded by a circle of tumbled stones.

'This is it,' said Merryn. 'Fang an t-Sithein, the Fank of the Fairies. It's exactly how Donald thought it would be.'

'What now?' Hamish whispered.

'Get down, hold onto his mane and keep a look out for the witch,' said Merryn.

'I'd rather stay on his back,' said Hamish. 'It feels safer.'

'Well you can't, and it isn't. If the witch spooks him you won't be able to stop him from running away. Get down. Talk to him and hang on for all you're worth.'

Hamish slipped down. 'I'm scared,' he said as his feet touched the ground. 'This place is spooky.'

'I know,' said Merryn. 'I can feel it too, but we can't stop now. We have to stay close together because we don't know how far the bubble will stretch.'

Taking a deep breath to steady herself she stepped towards the wall. If the Fairy Folk were as helpful as Roane, she would have nothing to fear. But she had been told twice that you can't be too careful where fairies are concerned. She put her palms together and closed her eyes.

'Please don't let me forget the words,' she whispered. She opened her eyes and took a tentative step through a gap between the tumbled stones.

Immediately, a voice called. 'Stop, proceed at your peril.'

Startled, she looked round. There was no-one to be seen. Kester nudged her with his nose, but before she could take another step, the voice came again, sharp and commanding.

'Stop and state your business.'

Merryn screwed up her eyes and tried to picture the words in the book. 'I...I come in peace,' she stammered. 'I...I come to ask assistance of the Fairy Folk. My Quest is to right a great wrong and without your help I am unable to proceed.'

There was no reply. The silence of the night was broken only by the distant murmur of the sea. Time passed. As seconds turned to minutes she grew more and more anxious. She stood first on one leg and then on the other. She chewed on her fingers. She put her arm round Hamish. She grasped Kester's mane, and she glanced fearfully around for signs of the witch. Thankfully the sky was undisturbed. The witch did not arrive, and at last, an order came.

'You may advance, mortal child.'

Taking Hamish firmly by the hand she moved into the circle. Immediately the voice spoke again.

'You must proceed alone.'

'No!' The thought of Hamish and Kester staying at the bottom of the mound while she went to the top almost paralysed her with fear. They had to stay together, all three of them, all the time. If the bubble didn't stretch to hold them all, anything could happen. Kester had the necklace. Without it her protection was diminished. The fairies might capture her. Without her, Hamish wouldn't be able to outwit the witch. She looked despairingly at Kester, shrugging her shoulders as if asking what she should do.

But Kester was already taking a backward step, and Hamish snatched his hand out of hers and gave her a push. 'Go on,' he urged.

The voice grew in impatience. 'If you do not come immediately, your chance will be lost.'

Merryn gulped down the lump that had risen in her throat. She stepped away, and with many a backward glance, she climbed to the top of the grassy slope. There she stopped and waited.

Nothing happened. What was she supposed to do? Nervously she went over the instructions. Of course! How could she have forgotten? She had to ring the bell. The sporran opened as if it had been waiting for her decision. She took out the bell and shook it. Three clear notes rang out. The sound trembled on the night air, and before it died away, a figure appeared on the rocky outcrop above her. She stared at the woman's round face, at her long green dress and crisp white apron.

'I know,' said the woman. 'You expected a dainty thing with wings like those of butterflies. Am I right?'

Merryn could find no words to answer. She merely nodded.

'Stuff and nonsense,' said the woman. 'No such thing. They are not fairies. They are imaginings, made up by people with no true knowledge. I am a Fairy, a real Fairy.'

She threw back her head and laughed. And although they were nowhere to be seen, Merryn knew that other fairies were listening, for their laughter rippled from the ground beneath her feet. It rose around her in waves of merriment, making a blush rise to her cheeks. The Fairy woman raised her hand and the laughter stopped as swiftly as it had started.

'Do not feel foolish,' she said. 'Your ignorance on the subject of Fairy Folk is understandable. There are few who know the truth, and even fewer who have the courage to seek us out. State your business for I have much to do, and your visit has interrupted more important matters.'

It was not the welcome Merryn had hoped for. She chewed on her lip and looked into the Fairy woman's eyes. But try as she would, she couldn't remember what she had to say.

'I...I've come to borrow,' she stammered.

The frown that settled on the Fairy woman's face made her realise her mistake. She stopped, thought hard and then repeated the words she'd memorised. 'I come in peace. I come to ask assistance of the Fairy Folk. My Quest is to right a great wrong and without your help I am unable to proceed.'

The Fairy woman glanced at Merryn's hand. 'From whom did you steal the silver bell?'

Merryn's voice rose indignantly. 'I did not steal it.'

The Fairy woman sneered. 'And you expect me to believe you?'

Merryn hesitated. There was something deeply unsettling about the Fairy woman's attitude. Calmly she unzipped her fleece and let the glow from the crystal pendulum shine out into the night. From the bottom of the mound, Kester whinnied softly. He could see it, but the Fairy woman did not react. Merryn's worst fears were confirmed. The Fairy woman could not be trusted.

'I did not steal the silver bell,' she repeated. 'It appeared in my bedroom as if by magic.'

'That is strange indeed.' The Fairy woman raised her eyebrows. 'Who told you to bring it to me? And how did you find your way to Fang an t-Sithein?'

Kester's Book had given her words to learn but it hadn't given an answer to these questions. She swallowed hard and tried to speak clearly. 'It was written in a book,' she said, 'and the horse brought me here.'

The Fairy woman walked right round her before stopping and staring into her eyes. Merryn grew hot and uncomfortable under the penetrating gaze, but she did not look away and she did not blink. Eventually the Fairy woman stepped down the mound and looked closely at Hamish and Kester. As she came back towards Merryn she rubbed her hands together thoughtfully.

'There is more to you than meets the eye. I see that you have magic power. Why you have it I do not know. But I know that you have faced great danger to arrive at my door. Your bravery is to be commended, especially in one so young. For that reason you may tell me what you want of me.'

'I ask that for two nights you loan to me the heart-stone so that I may use it to right the wrong.'

'Hah!' The Fairy woman threw up her hands and gave a scornful laugh. It echoed round the mound, and from deep underground came a burst of equally scornful laughter.

Merryn winced at the menacing sound. The crystals lay in the sporran at her waist. The crystal pendulum hung round her neck. But the necklace of sea-beans and hag-stones was with Kester. How much protection did she really have? Was she already outside the protective bubble? She had no way of knowing. How many fairies were there? And if they all turned against her would she be able to protect herself?

She glanced at Hamish and saw that he had buried his face in Kester's mane. She could sense his fear. She wanted to run back and reassure him, but the laughter had stopped and she dare not break the silence that followed.

Chapter 20

The Fairy woman turned a grave face towards Merryn. Her words, harsh and uncompromising cut through the air like a knife. 'You ask too much mortal child. The heart-stone is irreplaceable. You will have to bargain for the loan of it. What do you offer in return?'

'I will give you the silver bell to keep forever.'

The Fairy woman took the bell and shook it. As its clear notes rang out she smiled and spoke softly. 'It is a pretty thing to be sure, and the music it makes is sweet.'

Thinking that the bargain was sealed, Merryn sighed with relief. But it was not to be. When the Fairy woman spoke again, her voice had the ring of steel.

'It is not enough. What else do you bring?'

Merryn, stunned by the sudden change of tone, couldn't answer. The sporran had given her nothing but the silver bell. She had to think carefully until the words she'd memorised were needed.

'I have nothing else to give and without the heart-stone I cannot right the wrong.'

'Do not lie,' said the Fairy woman. 'Your horse has a necklace of peculiar power. Let him step forward. I must see it more closely.'

Merryn thought quickly. 'My brother will lead him, for they must stay together.'

The Fairy woman's eyes narrowed. 'Do not think that you can set the terms. The boy must stay outside.'

Merryn looked at Hamish. She had to put his safety first, but her heart sank at the thought of letting

Kester down. She was trying to decide what to do when Hamish took the decision from her.

He drew himself up to his full height. 'Go on,' he said. 'I can't see the witch. I'll be fine, honestly I will.'

'No! I can't risk it.' Merryn turned her back on the Fairy woman and started down the slope to join him.

'You anger me,' the Fairy woman called. 'You ask for help and then you walk away. I give you one last chance. Leave the boy outside the circle and let the horse step forward. If you do not obey, you will lose the bell and never see me more.'

Merryn kept on walking, but Hamish slapped Kester's rump. 'Go on,' he urged. 'We can't stop now.'

Kester trotted towards Merryn. He nudged her with his nose and pushed her back the way she'd come. She tried to step aside, but he was too quick for her and soon she found herself in front of the Fairy woman.

'The horse and the boy have more sense than you,' said the Fairy woman. 'They know it is unwise to disobey me.'

Merryn's concern was all for Hamish. He stood alone, down at the bottom of the mound, outside the circle of Fang an t-Sithein. The power of the necklace and the crystals may not reach him. She hardly heard the Fairy woman's words. Anxiously she scanned the sky. As yet, there was no sign of the witch, but if she arrived, Hamish would be an easy target.

'Take care,' said the Fairy woman. 'Forget your brother. A lapse of concentration could be your downfall. The sooner our business is completed the sooner you can join him.'

With a huge effort, Merryn turned back. The Fairy woman was looking at the necklace, and the glint of greed in her eyes was plain for all to see. It was obvious that she wanted it. But if she asked for it, Merryn knew that she would have to refuse. Without it, all three of them would be at the mercy of the witch.

'I repeat,' said the Fairy woman. 'The bell is not enough. You must give me something else of value.'

'The silver bell is all I have.' Merryn protested. 'I have nothing else to give.'

The Fairy woman grew angry. 'Nothing else to give,' she exclaimed.

Hidden from view, other fairies voiced their displeasure. The air around the mound began to vibrate with a malicious presence. Merryn glanced nervously at Hamish. His head was bowed and he had his hands over his ears as if he was trying to shut out the ominous sound.

She started to shout. 'Hamish, you must keep a look...'

'Silence,' snapped the Fairy woman. 'Forget your brother, and do not lie. You say you have nothing else to give, but I have already told you, your horse has a necklace of peculiar power. Give it to me and I will lend the heart-stone.'

'No,' Merryn replied. 'It is not mine to give.'

'Then I will take it.' The Fairy woman tried to snatch the necklace, but Kester tossed his head and stepped aside.

Merryn moved away too. Her mind was in turmoil. They were trapped between the witch's spells and the Fairy woman's refusal to accept the silver bell. Kester's Book had told her to speak with absolute honesty so that is what she had to do. Determinedly she faced the Fairy woman.

'The necklace is our protection,' she said. 'Without it our Quest will end and the witch will triumph. I cannot give it to you. It is not mine to give and you have no right to take it.'

The Fairy woman's face flared to an angry red.

Words flooded into Merryn's head. They gave her such a surge of confidence that she spoke without hesitation. 'I came to make a bargain,' she said, 'and the terms are these. In exchange for two night's loan of the heart-stone I will give the silver bell to you to keep for ever.'

'You displease me, mortal child, but...'

Before the Fairy woman could say more, a noise as of a wind whistling filled the air. Hamish screamed as the witch swooped down towards him. In an instant, Merryn and Kester forgot the Quest. They dashed down the mound. The bubble went with them. With scarce a second to spare it encompassed Hamish. As the witch collided with it, her broomstick bucked and faltered. With a yell of rage she swerved and urged it into the air.

'I'm sorry,' Merryn threw her arms round Hamish. 'We'll forget it.'

But the Fairy woman would not let them forget. She had followed them down the mound and her gaze was fixed on the necklace. 'Come back,' she ordered. 'I have not finished with you.'

Merryn held onto Hamish. 'Not without my brother.'

'Then let him step inside Fang an-t Sithein,' said the Fairy woman.

Merryn's heart seemed to freeze inside her chest. Donald had told her what happened to mortals who were lured into fairy mounds. She tried to scream a warning, but the words stuck in her throat.

The Fairy woman snapped her fingers, and a Fairy boy appeared beside her. 'He will take care of your brother,' she said with a smile.

As the boy held out his hand, Hamish stepped towards him.

Quickly, Merryn pulled him back. 'Never,' she cried. 'You will not take my brother, and you will not take the necklace.'

The Fairy woman turned away. 'Then it is your loss. I will not lend the heart-stone.'

Kester whinnied frantically. Merryn stood her ground. Something was telling her that the Fairy woman would not give up. She wanted the necklace and she would try to strike a different bargain. Even so, there were many anxious moments as she waited to see if she was right.

At the top of the mound, the Fairy woman paused. 'Let us not be hasty,' she said. 'Step forward and let the boy come with you. You spoke the truth about the danger of your situation. But I am mightily displeased that you brought that danger to my door.'

'I'm sorry,' said Merryn. 'The witch followed us, and when we leave she will leave too. Her quarrel lies with us, not with you.'

'You know nothing,' said the Fairy woman in a voice that was harsh with scorn. 'If I help you, she will wreak a terrible revenge on my people. We are in need of even more protection now. You must give me the necklace.'

'I cannot,' said Merryn. 'I told you, it is not mine to give. Besides, the witch has sworn to destroy all three of us, and without the necklace she will succeed. I ask again for two night's loan of the heart-stone. In exchange you may keep the silver bell for ever.'

The Fairy woman laughed. She shook her head and held up the silver bell. 'I already have it,' she said, 'and I will not return it.'

'That's not fair,' Hamish blurted out. 'That's stealing. You can't...'

Merryn gasped and pulled on his hand to silence him, but the look on the Fairy woman's face had already stopped his words.

'How dare you challenge me, mortal boy? And who said I had to be fair? I do what is best for my people. Besides, there is much that is unfair in your world so I do not see the need for such surprise.'

She turned to Merryn. 'It is foolhardy of your brother to criticise me. And yet, against my better judgement, I admire you both for your bravery. I am not without sympathy. Explain exactly why you need the heart-stone.'

'I would tell you if I knew,' said Merryn. 'But I cannot. I have not yet received instructions. I was sent to obtain the heart-stone and that is all I know.'

'Then I do not think I can help,' said the Fairy woman. 'But wait while I speak to my Council.' And she disappeared into the mound with the silver bell in her hand.

Chapter 21

Time passed. The Fairy woman did not return. Merryn glanced at her watch and struggled to hold back tears of frustration. Outside the ring of stones, the witch was flying, words rising and falling in a chant that tied Merryn's stomach in knots. Would the spell she was weaving break through the bubble? And if it did, what would happen next?

Her head filled with so many questions that it seemed ready to burst. Did Kester have to make his own way back to the post or would he be drawn back when the sun rose? Would the necklace disappear with him or would it be left on the post where the witch or the Fairy woman could find it?

She had no answers, but one thing was clear. She had to retrieve the necklace before Kester went back into the post. If she didn't, she and Hamish would be at the mercy of the witch. And without it, she would never be able to release Kester again. Worried that they would run out of time, she looked for signs of the Fairy woman's return. There were none.

She grabbed Hamish's hand. 'Come on,' she said. 'We have to go.'

'But we haven't got the heart-stone.'

'I know,' she said, 'but the witch is casting another spell. It's too dangerous to wait.'

Taking hold of Kester's mane she tried to lead him down the slope, but he strained against her. She leapt onto his back, pulled Hamish up behind her, and dug her heels into his flanks. Still he refused to move.

The witch stopped chanting. She flew high above the Fairy mound and stretched out her hands towards them. 'Burn,' she shouted, 'burn, burn. Horse and mortals, burn them all.'

A million tongues of flame lapped round Fang an-t Sithein, arching over their heads, crackling and roaring and reaching high into the sky. Kester neighed in terror and rushed towards the gap in the wall. He skidded to a halt, for there in front of them, was a wall of fire. He swung round, bucking and snorting.

'Keep going,' Merryn shouted. 'The flames can't get through the bubble. We can ride through them. I'm sure we can.'

'Go,' yelled Hamish. 'It's our only chance.'

Kester steadied himself, but before he could dash through the gap in the wall, dozens of spears hurtled through the air towards the witch. Caught unawares, she slipped from the broomstick, bounced off the bubble and tumbled to the ground. Her spell was broken. The flames died away. Screeching with fury, she picked herself up, hobbled to a boulder on the nearby hillside and began to chant another spell.

Hamish tugged at Merryn's arm. 'What do we do now?'

'You listen to me,' commanded the Fairy woman as she re-appeared on the rock above them. 'You have displeased me again. You should not have tried to leave. Our business was not finished and it would serve you right if I sent you away empty handed. However, my Council have made a decision and I am obliged to uphold it.'

Merryn didn't reply. She couldn't find the words. Her throat was so dry that her tongue was sticking to the roof of her mouth. She was afraid that the Fairy woman was about to make even more demands.

'Do not dismount,' said the Fairy woman. 'This will not take long. My Council agree that the silver bell is not enough. You must accept the tasks I set and you must return tomorrow at midnight.'

'We'll never make it,' Hamish protested.

The Fairy woman looked at him with narrowed eyes. 'Explain yourself, mortal boy.'

Hamish flinched. 'We...we can't release the horse until midnight,' he stammered, 'and we...we have a long way to come.'

The Fairy woman turned to Merryn. 'Is this true?' she demanded.

'Yes, it is true.'

'Then we will make it one o'clock. But I warn you, if you do not arrive on time, my soldiers will find you and they will take the necklace.'

Merryn looked at the Fairy woman with anxious eyes. 'But if we succeed, do you promise to loan the heart-stone for two nights?'

The Fairy woman inclined her head. 'If you succeed I will keep my word,' she said. 'Do you accept?'

Hamish grabbed Merryn's shoulder. 'We don't know what the tasks are,' he whispered. 'We can't accept. It's too risky.'

'It's our only chance,' she whispered back. And although her heart felt like a lead weight in her chest, she faced the Fairy woman squarely. 'We accept,' she said. 'You give us no choice.'

'Then mark my words, for I will say this once and once only. You must bring a necklace of sea-beans and hag-stones.' She nodded towards the necklace that hung round Kester's neck. 'As like to that as you can make it. Bring too, a paper bag containing nine times nine yellow periwinkles, and lastly, a garland of moon daisies gathered by moonlight and untouched by the morning sun.'

Merryn opened her mouth to protest, but the Fairy woman had disappeared.

'It's impossible!' Hamish exclaimed. 'We'll never do it.'

'Hush,' said Merryn. 'We must remember what she said. The first thing was a necklace of sea-beans and hag-stones as like to this as we can make it. Then there was something about periwinkles.

'Yellow ones in a paper bag,' said Hamish, 'but how many? She told us and I've forgotten.'

'Nine times nine,' said Merryn, 'that's eighty-one. But there were three things. What was the last one?' She closed her eyes and ran her fingers through her hair as she tried to remember.'

'I've got it,' said Hamish. 'It was moon daisies gathered by moonlight.'

'That's it,' said Merryn, 'and we have to make them into a garland.'

She looked up at the moonlit sky. 'It might be cloudy tomorrow so we must get them tonight. They grow on The Reef, and it's on our way home. Hurry, we've no time to lose.'

As soon as they left the Fairy mound, the witch flew above them, but to Merryn's surprise, she didn't try to stop them. Only when they reached The Reef and were ready to pick the moon daisies did she hurtle into action.

'Wind,' she screamed. 'Wind, come to my aid.'

Softly at first, a gentle breeze began to blow. Gradually it gained strength until it howled like a hurricane. It ploughed a furrow across The Reef uprooting moon daisies as it went. It buffeted the bubble and threatened to send it toppling and tumbling towards the sea.

Merryn pushed Kester. 'Down,' she said, 'lie down.'

As he rolled onto his side she dropped to her knees and pulled Hamish down beside her. With their heads close together they lay against Kester's flank. The wind grew wilder. The bubble swayed and rocked, but the wind did not enter it. Merryn watched as the witch struggled to control the broomstick. It was tossing like a kite in the teeth of the gale, jerking backwards and forwards as it dropped lower and lower.

'Ten thousand curses!' The witch screamed so loud that her voice carried above the roar of the wind. 'Fly straight. Fly high.' But the broomstick looped the loop and landed with a thud.

'Stop wind, stop,' she yelled. 'Enough, I say, enough!'

A sudden silence replaced the sound of the wind. The three of them got to their feet. Merryn stared in horror at the devastation around them. All the flowers lay bruised and battered, their stems broken, their petals strewn like snow.

'No moon daisies for you!' The witch laughed her hideous laugh, mounted her broomstick and flew away.

Merryn looked at the eastern sky. There was no sign of sunrise but she knew that soon the sky would take on a rosy glow. 'We'll be out of time if we're not careful,' she said. 'But we've got to get the moon daisies. They must grow somewhere else.'

'The loch side,' said Hamish. 'I've seen them there.'

Kester galloped to where the loch stretched silver in the moonlight. All along the shore, growing among the long grasses, were scatterings of moon daisies. They each picked a handful, and within minutes they were on their way again. But the sky was growing lighter.

'The moon daisies,' Merryn gasped. 'I mustn't let the sun shine on them, but I mustn't crush them either. I've nowhere to hide them.'

At her words, the sporran opened, the moon daises shrank and slipped inside, and the sporran closed itself. The moment they reached the post, the sun began to peep over the horizon. There was no time for words. Just before Kester was drawn into the post, Merryn grabbed the necklace.

'We made it,' she gasped, 'but we must hurry. I hope there'll be time for a sleep before Aunt Aggie wakes.'

Hamish groaned as they approached the cottage. Aunt Aggie was already up. She was standing in the middle of the lawn with her hands on her hips and a frown on her face. Her voice, sharp with anxiety, reached them long before they opened the gate.

'Where have you been and what time did you go out? You've had me worried sick.'

'Sorry,' said Merryn. 'We've only been for a walk. I'm not sure about the time. I didn't look at my watch.'

'We didn't want to waste such a lovely morning,' added Hamish. 'There are hares in the field and lapwings and....'

'That's as may be,' snapped Aunt Aggie. 'But I'm not pleased. Early morning walks are all very well, but I need to know exactly where you are. For the rest of the day you'll not leave the garden. Maybe that will teach you to heed my words.'

Hamish clenched his teeth and kicked the grass.

Merryn scowled. 'But Aunt Aggie...'

'Don't think you can get round me,' said Aunt Aggie. 'There'll be no going out this day, and I mean it.'

'We're stumped again,' Hamish said. 'We've got nothing but moon daisies. We'll never get periwinkles. As for finding hag-stones and sea-beans, we don't stand a chance.'

Chapter 22

'Aunt Aggie's the meanest woman in the world,' said Hamish as they reached the landing. 'We'll never get the things for the Fairy woman, and I promised Donald I'd help him in the garden today. Now I'll have to let him down.'

'Wait,' said Merryn. 'I'm sorry you can't help Donald, but it's not as bad as you think. We can...'

'That's just the point,' he shouted. 'We can't do anything. I wish we'd never come to this stupid island.' Muttering angrily about stupid witches and stupid fairies he went into his bedroom and slammed the door.

Merryn knew there was no point in trying to reason with him. Until he calmed down, she'd be better off on her own. There was a lot to do and she wasn't going to waste time waiting for him. She went into the cubbyhole and brought out the shell collection and the box of sea-beans and hag-stones. She laid them on her bed and thought about what else she would need.

If she'd been at home she would have found the things for herself. Here she would have to ask Aunt Aggie, but Aunt Aggie was already in a bad mood. Feeling very apprehensive, she went down to the kitchen. Aunt Aggie, standing at the table kneading dough, didn't even look up.

Merryn fumbled with her fingers and looked at the floor. 'Please, Aunt Aggie, may I borrow a tape measure, a needle and some thread?'

Aunt Aggie lifted her floury hands and sighed. 'I can't be looking now,' she said. 'Can't you see I'm busy? If you can't wait, just take my workbasket. Help yourself and mind you keep it tidy.'

'Thanks, Aunt Aggie, and please have you got any paper bags?'

'There are bags in the drawer by the sink.'

Merryn opened the drawer and searched through a heap of plastic bags. Underneath them, as if they'd been hoarded for a very long time, were a few brown paper bags. She chose the strongest, thanked Aunt Aggie again and took the workbasket to her room.

Everything she needed was ready. But where should she start? The sporran opened. The moon daisies appeared. They grew to their proper size, and to her relief, they looked as fresh as when they'd been picked. Kester's Book followed. It leapt out as if it had been waiting for her.

Follow the Fairy woman's instructions exactly
and remember that in everything,
Fairy Folk favour multiples of three.
Moon daisies picked by moonlight
and untouched by morning sun will not wilt,
but you must take care
not to crush a single flower.

Taking the bunch of moon daisies, she cut the stems and made a slit in each one. The three times table went through her head as she worked, and once she'd decided on the number twenty-seven, threading the flowers didn't take long. It was much easier than making a chain of ordinary daisies. When the garland was finished she laid it carefully in a drawer where the sun couldn't reach it.

She opened the box of shells and had started to sort the yellow periwinkles into the lid when Hamish poked his head round the door.

'I want to go home,' he said. 'I hate it here. It's not a holiday at all. All we've done is try to save Kester, and now Aunt Aggie's grounded us, we can't even do that.'

'I think we can,' Merryn replied. 'I tried to tell you, but you wouldn't listen. I've made the moon daisy garland and look what I found. She shook the box lid so that the yellow periwinkles rattled. 'Come on, this is something you can do.'

Looking slightly more cheerful, he pushed his hands in among the limpets and cockle shells. One by one he picked out the yellow periwinkles and counted them into the lid. 'That's seventy one,' he said. He scrabbled more and more frantically as fewer and fewer came to light. 'I've only got seventy-eight and there aren't any more.' He looked at Merryn with worried eyes. 'What do we do now?'

'Count them again to see if you've missed any.'

This time he counted out loud, slowly and carefully. 'I was right. It's still seventy-eight.'

There were no more in the box. Together they counted them into the paper bag and agreed that they were still three short.

'Bother,' said Merryn. 'We'll have to find some on the way tonight. It'll slow us down, but there's nothing else for it, unless Aunt Aggie changes her mind and lets us go out.'

'She won't do that,' said Hamish. 'You heard what she said. We're grounded until tomorrow. Anyway, I don't know why you're bothering. The Fairy woman asked for three things. There's no point in turning up with two. If we can't make the necklace we're stumped.'

'But we can make it,' said Merryn. 'Look what else I found.'

She opened the box of sea-beans and hag-stones and thrust it towards him. His face broke into a grin. He picked out the sea-beans and put them on the lid.

'I'll make the holes,' he said. 'There's a hand drill in the tool box in the shed. I've been hoping to use it.'

'Don't go yet,' said Merryn as she took off the necklace. 'We have to copy this one so we need to look at it really carefully.' She counted the sea-beans and hag-stones. 'They're in three groups of three. That's nine of each. Kester's Book said that Fairy Folk favour multiples of three, so it's perfect.'

Hamish took the necklace from her and peered at it through his magnifying glass. 'The cord has three strands too,' he said. 'I think they're plaited. Here, take a look.'

'You're right,' said Merryn, 'and there are three knots between the groups. You go and drill nine sea-beans while I sort out the hag-stones and find some thread.'

Smiling broadly, Hamish went off to the shed. Merryn chose nine hag-stones before searching Aunt Aggie's workbasket. Among the reels of cotton she found a ball of thread that looked ideal. Plaiting would be easier if Hamish could help. So after she'd cut three lengths of thread and tied them together, she went to see how he was getting on with the drilling.

When she opened the shed door her heart sank. Hamish looked up from a litter of broken sea-beans.

She opened her mouth to tell him to be more careful, but he stopped her with a glare.

'Don't say a word,' he snapped as the drill slipped and another sea-bean shattered. 'Just go away. I'm doing my best. I've drilled seven, and you're making me nervous.'

Merryn backed away. 'Please, please don't break any more,' she whispered.

Far too worried to go back to her room, she leaned against the shed wall. She listened anxiously to the sound of the drill and wondered just how many sea-beans he'd broken.

Eventually Hamish came out and glowered at her. 'What are you waiting for? I don't need you watching me all the time.' He marched past and went into the cottage.

Merryn chased after him. 'When I saw how many you'd smashed I was scared we wouldn't have enough.'

'Well we have, so there!' He slammed nine sea-beans onto the bed next to the hag-stones.

'That's great,' she said. 'Well done. Now we've got everything we need.' She handed him the knotted end of the cotton. 'Here, hold this tight while I do the plaiting.'

As soon as the plait was finished, Hamish snatched it from her. 'I think it's too thick,' he said. 'It'll never go through the sea-beans.'

'Then you should have made bigger holes,' said Merryn.

'There's nothing wrong with the holes,' he said. 'I drilled them so I'm going to thread them.' He turned away and took a knitting needle from Aunt Aggie's workbasket. 'I can push the plait through with this.'

'Don't!' Merryn tried to snatch the knitting needle. 'It's too thick. Stop it, Hamish. Stop!'

He elbowed her out of the way, caught the plait on the point of the knitting needle, and forced it into the hole. There was a splintering sound. A crack ran from one side of the sea-bean to the other. He groaned as the two halves fell apart.

'Oh! Hamish,' Merryn cried. 'Why don't you listen? Now you'll have to drill another one.'

He hung his head and didn't answer.

'Hamish, go and drill another one.'

He didn't move.

She gave him a push. 'Go on, get a move on. Go and drill another one.'

'I can't,' he whispered. 'I broke them all.'

'You didn't!' Merryn's heart missed a beat. 'Tell me it isn't true.'

Hamish slid off the bed onto the floor and choked on a sob.

Chapter 23

Merryn thumped the bed with her fist and shouted. 'How could you be so stupid? Do you realise what you've done?' She stood up and paced round the room. 'If we can't make a new necklace it'll be the end of everything.'

She clasped and unclasped her hands. She shook her head and chewed on her knuckles. 'The Fairy woman will take the necklace. Kester will stay in the post for ever.' Her voice rose and wavered. 'And the witch...she'll...' She gulped and her voice fell to a whisper. 'She'll catch us and she'll...' Unable to put the terrifying thoughts into words she faltered and stopped.

Hamish looked up. He stared at her with wide anxious eyes. 'I...I didn't think... I...I thought I...could...' His face crumpled and his sobs turned to a howl of real distress.

Merryn tried to push away the horror of what the witch would do. For a long time she was silent. The only sound in the room came from Hamish as he sobbed and sniffed. She couldn't bear to see his shaking shoulders and heaving chest. Gradually, feelings of guilt overtook those of fear and anger. She was supposed to be looking after him, and she'd done the opposite. It was her fault that they were mixed up in magic. She slid down beside him and put her arm round his shoulders.

'Come on, Hamish,' she said. 'I'm sorry I was mad. It's just that I'm worried about what's going to happen. I know you didn't break the sea-beans on purpose.

We've got to pull ourselves together. We can't sit here weeping and wailing and giving up. We've got to think of something or we won't get the heart-stone.'

When Hamish eventually managed to speak, his voice was very small, and it was punctuated by snuffles. 'We'd better make the necklace with what we've got. The Fairy woman didn't say how many sea-beans we had to use. Maybe eight will be enough.'

'I don't think so,' said Merryn. 'It has to be a copy of this one and eight isn't a multiple of three.'

'We could use six,' he said.

Merryn shook her head. 'No, it has to be nine.' She picked up the two halves of the broken sea-bean, and fitted them together. 'If we can't find another one I'll glue this, but I'm afraid she'll notice. Come on, I'll start threading and you can help me.'

She passed the plaited cotton through the eye of a long needle and checked that it would go through the holes in the sea-beans. 'If we start with hag-stones,' she said, 'we'll end with sea-beans. So we can finish it except for the last one. After that I don't know what we'll do.'

They worked together, threading and knotting, carefully measuring the spaces between the knots, always following the pattern of the original necklace. They had to stop for lunch, and the afternoon was almost over by the time they'd attached the eighth sea-bean.

'It's my fault that we're one short,' said Hamish, 'so I ought to find another one. I'm going to ask Aunt Aggie if she has any.'

'There's no point,' said Merryn. 'I know exactly what she'll say.'

'Well I'll ask anyway,' he said, 'only I'm scared she'll be mad at me.' He grabbed Merryn's hand. 'Come with me, please.'

They went downstairs together. The back door was open and Aunt Aggie was in the garden taking washing off the line.

'Aunt Aggie,' said Hamish. 'I don't suppose you have any sea-beans lying around.'

'Indeed I do not,' said Aunt Aggie. 'I don't hold with such superstitious nonsense.' Without another word she picked up her laundry basket and went indoors.

'I told you,' said Merryn.

Hamish scowled. He kicked at the gravel on the path, and at that moment Donald came out of his cottage and leaned over the fence.

'Well now,' he said. 'I thought you were coming to help me this morning. What happened?'

'Aunt Aggie grounded us for going out without telling her,' Hamish grumbled. 'And we're not allowed out of the garden or down the beach or anywhere.'

'Seems a bit harsh,' said Donald, 'but don't tell Aggie I said so. And what about you, young lady, have you found anything else of interest?'

'Not really,' said Merryn. 'We had to stay in so we've been trying to make a necklace of sea-beans and hag-stones, but we haven't got enough sea-beans.'

'And we'll never find any more,' added Hamish. He looked expectantly at Donald. 'I don't suppose you have any?'

'I used to have a few,' said Donald, 'but it's a long time since I set eyes on them.' He smiled at Merryn. 'I'd really like to see what you've been making.'

Merryn felt a sudden flicker of hope. She ran back into the cottage and returned a couple of minutes later with the necklace in her hand.

Donald took it from her and looked at it carefully. 'This is truly amazing,' he said. 'The design has the look of something really authentic. Where did you get the idea for the pattern? And why did you do everything in threes?'

Not wanting to give too much away, Merryn shrugged. 'I read that three was a magical number.'

'It certainly is,' said Donald, 'and it would be a terrible shame to leave such a wonderful necklace unfinished for the want of a single sea-bean. Let me think now. I'm not sure where to start looking, but give me half an hour and I'll see what I can do.'

As he turned into his cottage, Hamish called after him, 'I don't suppose you have any yellow periwinkles. We could do with some of those as well.'

Donald shook his head. 'Sorry, I gave my shell collection to my grandson years ago.'

'Nice try,' said Merryn, 'but we can find periwinkles for ourselves. It's the sea-bean I'm bothered about. Let's hope he can find one.'

There was nothing else to do. They went upstairs and sat on the bed as they waited anxiously to hear from Donald. Time after time Merryn checked her watch. 'I can't wait any longer,' she said. 'Waiting drives me mad. Let's go outside.'

There was no sign of Donald so they kicked a football around. After ten minutes, breathless and impatient they leaned on the fence and waited for him to appear. Merryn crossed her fingers, closed her eyes and wished and wished for another sea-bean. Five more minutes passed. Her fingers started to ache from being crossed for so long, but she wasn't going to uncross them for anything. Two minutes later the door opened and Donald came out with a smile on his face.

'You're in luck,' he said. 'Hold out your hands.' He placed a neatly drilled sea-bean on each of their upturned palms.

'You're brilliant!' Hamish jumped up and down with delight. 'Thank you, thank you, thank you.'

Merryn was so overcome with relief that she could barely speak. 'Thank you so much,' she whispered. 'We're really, really grateful.'

'We've got one, and we've got one to spare,' Hamish sang gleefully as they returned to the bedroom.

'Don't get carried away,' she said. 'We've done well, but we haven't got the heart-stone yet. There are still lots of things that can go wrong.'

'You mean like the witch stopping us from getting Kester out of the post?'

'Yes, and stopping us from getting to Fang an t-Sithein by one o'clock.'

'We'll do it,' said Hamish. 'At least we'll have all the things the Fairy woman asked for. I bet she'll be surprised. I bet she never thought we could do it.'

As soon as Merryn had threaded the ninth sea-bean, she tied the last three knots. 'Now,' she said, 'this is the tricky bit.' With great care, she used a fine needle to stitch the three raw ends from the beginning of the necklace into the knot at the end. It was finished.

Hamish picked it up. 'It's pretty neat,' he said. 'The last knot's a bit bigger than the others, but maybe she won't notice.'

'I'm afraid she will,' said Merryn, 'but I've done my best and I can't do any more.'

She held up the two necklaces, one in each hand. Apart from the newness of the thread, they looked remarkably similar. She put the original necklace back round her neck, and as she did so, Kester's Book opened and the invisible pen began to write.

You have done well.
Now put the new necklace
and the bag of periwinkles into the sporran.
But do not forget
that you are three periwinkles short.

'They'll never fit,' said Hamish.

'I bet they will,' said Merryn. 'Don't forget, this is magic.'

She was right. As she pushed the necklace towards the sporran, it became smaller and slipped itself inside. The bag of periwinkles followed.

Now, add the ball of thread
and a tape measure.

'But they belong to Aunt Aggie,' said Merryn. 'We can't just take them.'

'And we can't ask,' said Hamish. 'She'll want to know why we need them. Then we'll have to tell her everything and she'll still say no.'

You do not have a choice.
Your very lives may depend on taking them.
You must do as I bid you.

'You'd better put them in,' said Hamish.

Merryn closed her eyes to block out the words. How could their lives depend on a tape measure and a ball of thread? She had no idea, but she obeyed the instructions. Her hand shook as she pushed the two items towards the sporran. Like the necklace and the bag of periwinkles, they began to shrink, and when they were very tiny they too slipped inside.

More words appeared, words that made Hamish gasp. Words that made Merryn clench her fists so hard that her fingernails dug into her palms.

Not only must you outwit the witch
you must beware of the Fairy woman.
She is not to be trusted.
She intends to get the better of you.
If you do not stand your ground
she will succeed.

Chapter 24

Merryn knew that there wouldn't be a minute to spare if they were to reach Fang an-t Sithein by one o'clock. So she set the alarm for twenty past eleven. They needed to be standing by the post at midnight, ready for Kester's call.

'Get a move on,' she said as she prodded Hamish with her foot. 'And look, there's no sign of the moon. We were right to collect the moon daisies last night.'

She put the garland round her neck where it was least likely to get crushed. And within minutes, armed with torches, they were heading into the darkness. Thankfully, there was no sign of the witch. But when they reached the field, Merryn stopped and stared in horror. Kester's post was no longer alone. All around it stood a circle of other posts.

Hamish flashed his torch. 'Crumbs,' he said. 'How are we going to get past that lot?'

'I don't know,' said Merryn. 'But we've got to find a way.'

'It's OK,' said Hamish as they drew closer. 'Look, there are gaps.' He turned sideways and tried to squeeze between them.

'Something's blocking my way,' he squealed as he tried to push his way through. 'They're joined together by magic. It's impossible.'

Merryn set her shoulder against one of the posts. She pushed as hard as she could, but it wouldn't move. She stepped back and tried to fight the panic that was making her heart race.

'Magic to undo magic,' said Hamish. 'Let's try the crystals.'

Her hands shook so much that when the sporran opened, Hamish had to take them out. He tried to push them between the fence posts, but they bounced back.

'They're not helping,' he wailed. 'Try the necklace.'

Merryn reached for the necklace of sea-beans and hag-stones, but the moon daisies were in the way. Carefully she took off the garland and popped it over Hamish's head. Then she pulled off the necklace and dropped it over the first post. Hamish kicked the space on either side, but the invisible barrier did not give way. Merryn picked up the necklace and put it back on.

She grabbed the post and tried to shake it. 'Please, somebody, help us,' she begged.

The only response was Kester's frantic neigh.

'It's midnight,' she gasped. 'We're wasting time. Think of something else.'

'The book,' Hamish yelled. 'Ask Kester's Book.'

The sporran opened, the book leapt out and Hamish shone his torch onto a blank page.

'Hurry,' Merryn pleaded. 'Tell us what to do.'

The message that appeared was short and to the point.

Try the crystal pendulum
followed by the necklace.

'Crystal pendulum?' Hamish's eyebrows knitted together in a frown. 'What's it on about?'

'This,' said Merryn as she lifted it out of her fleece.

'I can't see it,' said Hamish. 'It's leaving me out again. It's not fair.'

'Never mind that now,' she snapped. 'You'll just have to trust me.'

Merryn's confidence returned as waves of colour flowed out into the night. The pendulum, dangling from her finger above one of the posts, settled into a rhythm. It circled slowly. Then it gathered speed until the colours merged in a halo of startling white light. For a whole minute it whizzed around its chosen path. Then it gradually slowed, and as soon as it stopped, Merryn dropped the necklace over the post.

Immediately, there came a crackling sound. She pulled Hamish back as showers of sparks flew into the air. The post hissed and sizzled, balls of coloured fire shot upwards and exploded above their heads. The barrier between the posts was no longer invisible. It curled and shrivelled as blue flames passed along it to the posts on either side. Like a spent firework, the first post fizzled and died.

'Yes!' Hamish shouted. 'It's working.'

Merryn pushed through the first gap to fling the necklace over the wooden horse's head. All around her, blue flames passed from post to post. As each one ignited, sparks and balls of fire filled the air. And when the last post was nothing more than a tiny charcoal stump, Kester stepped out of the whirl of coloured threads and whinnied in welcome.

'Hurry,' she said as they mounted. 'To Fang an t-Sithein as fast as you can.'

'No,' shouted Hamish. 'We've got to stop for the periwinkles. Go to the rocks at the end of Gott Bay.'

The sound of Kester's whinny sped across the island to the souterrain. It entered the witch's ears like the thrust of a dagger. She screamed and writhed about in an agony of disbelief. She wailed and tore her hair, and it was not until she'd exhausted herself that she fell back on her makeshift bed and wept hot tears of anger.

A few minutes earlier she'd heard Kester's desperate midnight cry. She'd smiled smugly in the certain knowledge that she had blocked the way to his post. She sat up and tried to understand her failure.

'Did I forget something? Did I leave something out?' She went over and over the spell in her head.

'No,' she fumed. 'I didn't forget a thing. I underestimated the power of those pesky children. Someone is helping them. Sea-beans and hag-stones would not have broken through my barrier. There is something even more powerful. I must find it and make it my own.'

She leapt to her feet. 'What am I thinking? Even now they'll be on their way to Fang an t-Sithein, and if the Fairy Folk side with them, my task will be even harder.'

Hoping to catch up with them before they reached the fairy mound, she grabbed her broomstick, crawled out of the souterrain and headed into the night.

On went Kester, galloping over The Reef and along Gott Bay. At the far end, he stopped and they slid from his back to look for periwinkles. Hamish shone his torch while Merryn scrabbled among the heaps of shells that had gathered between the rocks. There were plenty of periwinkles but yellow ones were hard to find.

'There's one,' said Hamish, 'and another.'

Merryn picked them up and went on searching. She couldn't find any more. 'Quick. Try somewhere else,' she said.

Hamish swung the torch beam around, bent down and held up the final yellow periwinkle. The sporran opened and the paper bag unfolded itself.

'We've got seventy-eight,' said Merryn, and she counted as she dropped the three new shells inside. 'Seventy-nine, eighty, eighty-one, that's it.' Carefully, she folded the top of the bag and it slipped itself back into the sporran.

The witch was nowhere to be seen. Unhindered by her, they made good progress, and soon they turned into the field that led to the fairy mound. Kester slowed to a canter and Merryn glanced at her watch. It was six minutes to one.

'Well done,' she said. 'We've made it.'

'No, you haven't,' screamed the witch as she hurtled towards them and collided with the bubble.

Although it didn't burst, the force of the impact dented it and the witch crashed into Kester's flanks. With nothing but the thin skin of the bubble between them, Hamish was knocked off balance. He lost his grip, slid sideways and tumbled to the ground.

'Stop,' Merryn shouted. 'We've lost Hamish.'

Kester skidded to a halt and trotted back to where Hamish was struggling to his feet. The witch turned in a sweeping curve and headed back towards them. Merryn pulled Hamish up onto Kester's back just as the witch crashed into them for the second time. Kester didn't falter. The witch howled a string of curses. She swung round again, gathered speed and zoomed in for a third attempt. Just before she reached them, Kester swerved and dashed through the gap in the wall. They'd made it. They were inside the ring of stones and there were two minutes to spare.

'I'll get you when you come out,' snarled the witch as she sat down on a boulder just outside the boundary wall. 'I don't care how long I have to wait. I'll be here and I'll get you. That's a promise.'

Merryn turned her back on the witch. They would have to face her later. Right now the Fairy woman was tapping her foot impatiently.

'Follow me,' Merryn whispered to Hamish, 'and keep hold of Kester.'

As they reached the top of the mound, the Fairy woman held Merryn in a chilling gaze. 'You insult me,' she said. 'You have brought your brother and the horse without my permission. I summoned you. I did not summon them. They must remain outside the circle.'

Merryn faced the Fairy woman bravely. Inside she was shaking, but she was determined to stand firm. She had brought the necklace, the periwinkles and the moon daisies, and she gambled on the fact that the Fairy woman wanted them.

'We are a team,' she said. 'We are in this together and if they have to leave, I will leave too.'

'Then the horse's necklace will be mine,' the Fairy woman said. 'Surely, you have not forgotten our agreement. Think carefully before you decide. Either you send your companions outside the circle, or my soldiers will surround the horse and take the necklace from him. Which is it to be?'

Chapter 25

Merryn stared into the Fairy woman's eyes with an unwavering gaze. 'All three of us will remain inside the circle.'

Kester's ears twitched. He nuzzled her neck and rested his nose on her shoulder. Hamish held Kester's mane with one hand and Merryn's sleeve with the other. The Fairy woman began to walk round them. She bristled with anger, but they did not flinch. When she stood before them once more, all three of them held their heads high and looked into her eyes.

The Fairy woman drew in her breath. 'You are stubborn and insolent,' she said. 'You anger me, for you do not give the respect that is my due. I have a mind to cancel our agreement.

Kester rolled his eyes. He pawed the ground and snorted. Hamish let go of Kester and Merryn. He clenched his fists and took a step towards the Fairy woman.

'I say that would be unworthy of you,' said Merryn. 'Last night you allowed my brother and the horse to stand before you. You spoke to all three of us. You did not say the tasks were for me alone. We have worked together and we have returned with the things you requested.'

The Fairy woman's eyebrows rose. She was obviously surprised. 'All of them?'

'Yes, we have brought them all.'

'Then I am honour bound to consider them,' said the Fairy woman. 'But if they do not meet my requirements I will be obliged to refuse them.' She snatched the garland of moon daisies from Hamish's neck. 'This was not meant for a mere mortal,' she snapped, 'and definitely not for a boy. It should not have been worn.'

'I beg your pardon,' said Merryn. 'We did not know how else to carry it. Our main concern was to avoid crushing the flowers.'

'Hmm!' The Fairy woman examined them carefully. 'You succeeded in that, but who told you how many moon daisies to include?'

'No-one,' Merryn replied. 'It was my own idea. I worked it out for myself.'

The Fairy woman frowned. 'I do not believe you. Explain your reasoning, and take care, for if you lie, you risk everything.'

Merryn did not flinch. 'I risk nothing,' she said, 'because I speak the truth. I know that Fairy Folk favour number three. I also know that three threes are nine, and that three nines are twenty-seven. That is why I chose the number.'

'You are unlike other mortals,' said the Fairy woman. 'Against my better judgement I believe you. By choosing twenty-seven you have shown great wisdom. Therefore I will accept the moon daisies.'

At her words, a Fairy man appeared. The Fairy woman placed the garland on the green velvet cushion that he held before him.'

'Now I will take the necklace,' she said.

Quickly, Hamish stood between Merryn and the Fairy woman. He cupped his hands round the sporran and whispered. 'Don't let her see the light from the crystals,'

The sporran opened, Merryn took out the necklace and handed it over. As the Fairy woman passed it through her fingers her face creased in a frown. Merryn thought of the hours they had spent in making it. She lifted her chin defiantly, but she twisted her fingers anxiously as the Fairy woman's frown deepened.

'It is as you asked.' Merryn tried to speak with confidence. 'It is a copy of the other necklace. There are nine sea-beans and nine hag-stones.' She paused and took a breath. 'They are threaded in groups of three, there are three knots between the groups, and the thread is plaited from three strands.'

'That is as may be.' The Fairy woman looked at the knots for a long time. Then she thrust the necklace at Merryn. 'But it will not do.'

Merryn put her hands behind her back and refused to take it. She screwed up her eyes to force back tears of disappointment. Stand your ground. The words from Kester's Book appeared as if they were engraved on the inside of her eyelids. She took courage from them and spoke out bravely.

'A necklace of sea beans and hag-stones as like to that as you can make it. Those were your very words. We have done exactly as you asked. To reject it would be dishonourable.'

Shocked at Merryn's words, the Fairy woman lurched backwards. Out of the hill came a gasp as if a hundred Fairy Folk had drawn in their breath. The Fairy woman's eyes flashed with anger. She threw the necklace at Merryn's feet and walked away.

The witch mounted her broomstick, rose into the air and whirled round the ring of stones. 'Bravo!' she called before returning to the boulder in fits of wild laughter.

A sudden surge of panic filled Merryn's chest. She had said too much. She must apologise before the Fairy woman disappeared. She opened her mouth to call her back, to ask forgiveness for her rudeness, but no words came out. Bewildered, she closed her eyes and tried to think. The words appeared exactly as before. Stand your ground.

'Wait,' she called. 'Our business is not finished. We have kept our side of the bargain. We made the necklace and we deserve to know why it is unacceptable.'

'We,' exclaimed the Fairy woman. 'Your brother helped you? Then I will tell him too. The workmanship is flawed. The knots are badly tied. I can see where the cotton was joined. It is untidily done. What say you to that, mortal boy?'

Hamish, made bold by Merryn's stance, didn't hesitate. 'I say we did our best. You told us to make it like the other one, and that's what we've done. You didn't say it had to be perfect.'

The Fairy woman inclined her head as if she could not disagree. 'I will allow you that,' she said. 'It is true. Therefore, I will reconsider.'

Voices from deep within the hill grew animated. Merryn strained to catch what they were saying. There seemed to be a verbal battle between those who wanted the Fairy woman to accept the necklace, and those who wanted her to refuse it.

The argument must have reached the witch's ears, for she came close to the wall of tumbled stones. Raising her voice above the others she cried out.

'Refuse, I tell you, refuse. If you accept I will destroy you and your people.'

Merryn looked from the Fairy woman to the witch and back again. A feeling of hopelessness washed over her. Surely, the Fairy woman would refuse the necklace. She would never risk the safety of her own people for the sake of two mortal children and a horse.

The Fairy woman walked down the mound and jabbed her finger in the witch's direction. 'Do not threaten me,' she cried. 'I do not wish to do battle with you. But it is for me to decide my course of action. I will not let your words influence me. This is my business and I suggest you keep your long nose out of it.'

Turning her back on the screaming witch she returned to Merryn. 'I cannot accept the necklace as it is,' she said. 'It will have to be re-threaded. You must return at the same time tomorrow with a ball of thread.'

Merryn saw the ghost of a smile twitching at the corners of the Fairy woman's lips. You are trying to trick us, she thought. You just want the original necklace. You set tasks that you thought were impossible. Well, we have succeeded and now you don't know how to get out of the bargain.

The Fairy woman picked up the necklace and stared at the one round Kester's neck. She seemed to be checking that the patterns were indeed the same. The sporran opened and Merryn cautiously slipped her hand inside. In the second it took to lift out the ball of thread, light from the crystals glowed from the opening. The Fairy woman's head jerked round. She glanced at the sporran, but it had already closed itself and the glow had faded.

Savouring her moment of triumph, Merryn held out the ball of thread. 'We do not need to return tomorrow. I believe this is what you require.'

The Fairy woman opened her mouth and closed it again. It was obvious that she was lost for words. Several seconds passed before she spoke. 'You have The Gift,' she said. 'I do not know how you came by it, for it is not of the mortal world.' She took the ball of thread, unrolled it a little and tugged to test the strength of it. Slowly she nodded her head.

'I cannot overlook the shoddy workmanship,' she said, 'but now that we have the design, my seamstress will be able to re-thread the necklace. Some of my people will be displeased with my decision, but you have completed the task and I am honour bound to accept.'

Immediately, a second Fairy man appeared. The Fairy woman placed the necklace and the ball of cotton on his green velvet cushion. From beneath the hill came the sound of applause, but an undercurrent of muttered disapproval threatened to deaden it.

'If you ignore the witch you will put all our lives at risk,' said the first Fairy man.

'But a bargain made should be a bargain honoured,' said the second.

'What care we for mortal children and a horse,' shouted someone from within the hill. 'Why should we help them? What have mortals ever done for us?'

Another voice, louder and more insistent, rose above the others. 'Let the witch have them.'

Voice after voice joined in. The chant grew louder as more and more Fairy Folk added to the sound. Kester reared, snorted and bared his teeth. Hamish clung to Merryn. She put her arms round him and held him tight as the words reverberated round the mound.

'Let the witch have them. Let the witch have them.'

Chapter 26

The Fairy woman raised her hand. As the chanting died away, silence fell and she turned to Merryn. 'You see my dilemma. My people are divided in their opinion. Tell me, what would you do in my place?'

The words that came into Merryn's head were not the ones she wanted to say. But she couldn't hold them back. 'I would look after my own,' she said.

'Don't say that,' Hamish gasped. 'How can you say that?'

'So you advise me to let the witch have you,' said the Fairy woman.

Merryn struggled to keep her voice from shaking. 'It is not my place to advise you. It is for you to decide, but I hope that you can find another way. The witch is evil. She has done a great wrong and we are trying to put it right. We do not deserve...' She gulped and caught her breath. 'We do not deserve to die at her hands.'

The Fairy woman inclined her head. 'Brave words and honest too,' she said, 'and I am inclined to agree. But I need time to consider.'

Outside the circle, the witch shook her fist and screamed. She rose on her broomstick and swooped low over Fang an t-Sithein. 'Accept the periwinkles,' she yelled, 'and we will be at war.'

The shouts from the Fairy mound rose again. So many voices filled the night air that it was impossible to make out what they were saying.

'Silence,' the Fairy woman commanded, 'and that means you too.' She pointed at the witch and turned back to Merryn.

'The decision falls on me alone,' she said. 'I do not take it lightly, but I made a bargain and I must honour it.' She held out her hand. 'So give me the periwinkles.'

When the sporran opened, Merryn forgot to cover the opening with her hand. The crystals sent out flashes of light. Horrified, she pulled out the paper bag as quickly as she could. But was she too late? The Fairy woman's eyes were glinting greedily. Had she seen the light? Did she know there were crystals in the sporran? Was she about to ask for them too?

'The periwinkles,' repeated the Fairy woman. 'I am waiting and I grow impatient.'

She hadn't asked for anything else. Faint with relief, Merryn held out the paper bag. As the Fairy woman snatched it, two more Fairy men appeared. One carried a stool while the other held a silver bowl. The Fairy woman sat on the stool, placed the bowl in her lap, and put her hand inside the bag. 'One,' she said as she dropped the first periwinkle into the bowl, 'two, three, four, five...'

On and on she went until she reached eighty. There she stopped, peered into the paper bag, turned it upside down and shook it. 'Either you do not know the nine times table or your counting is faulty. Whichever is true, it has lost you the heart-stone.'

Merryn was shocked at the deliberate lie. Was there no end to the Fairy woman's trickery? 'There are eighty-one,' she insisted. 'I counted them many times.'

'And I did too,' added Hamish. 'There are eighty-one. You didn't count them properly, you...'

The Fairy woman silenced him with a look so fierce that he cringed and backed away.

'How dare you contradict me?' she snapped. 'There are but eighty. It will not do.'

'There are eighty-one,' repeated Merryn.

'There are eighty-one,' echoed Hamish.

Kester pawed the ground and snorted as if in agreement.

'Then one has fallen from the bag into your sporran.'

'That is not possible,' said Merryn. 'The bag was closed carefully.'

The Fairy woman stepped closer. 'Do not contradict me,' she said. 'I insist that you check.'

Merryn turned away. She half expected the sporran to remain closed, but it had already opened. She slipped her hand inside. She felt the crystals and she passed her fingers round the curved seam. The periwinkle was not there. The sporran closed itself. She lifted her chin defiantly and looked straight into the Fairy woman's eyes.

'It is not in the sporran. Please, I beg of you, count the periwinkles again.'

The Fairy woman's face turned red with rage. 'You ask too much. Empty the sporran. I must check for myself.'

'Empty the sporran,' chanted a hundred Fairy voices. 'Empty the sporran.'

The chant grew louder. Merryn covered her ears to block out the sound, but it grew and grew until the whole mound vibrated to its rhythm. In obvious distress, Kester snorted, pranced and rolled his eyes. Hamish, hanging onto his mane with both hands, struggled to keep him still. Merryn's mind whirled. She had to do something, but if she emptied the sporran the Fairy woman would want everything that was inside it.

It was all becoming too risky. They would not only lose the crystals, they would lose Kester's Book. Without it there would be no way of receiving instructions. They would have to forget the heart-stone and find another way of saving Kester.

'Come on, we're leaving,' she said to Hamish. 'We don't stand a chance when the rules keep changing.'

Determinedly, she leapt onto Kester's back and pulled Hamish up behind her. They set off down the mound, but before they reached the gap in the wall, three Fairy soldiers blocked their way. Looking frantically for another way out, Merryn urged Kester round the mound. With every step he took, another Fairy soldier appeared. Standing to attention, they formed a circle around the bottom of the mound.

'Empty the sporran,' they chanted. Their voices rose in pitch, so sharp and strident that Merryn thought her brain would burst.

'Empty the sporran.' The witch circled the mound, adding her screeching voice to the chant of the Fairy Folk.

Kester, snorting and shaking his head, bucked and bolted. He charged back to the top of the mound and reared so suddenly that Merryn and Hamish lost their grip. They slid over his rump and landed in a tangle at the feet of the Fairy woman. The chanting stopped. Gales of laughter filled the air, and the witch pointed her finger and joined in the merriment.

The Fairy woman raised her hand to stop the laughter. 'Now,' she said in a voice that chilled the air, 'you will empty the sporran.'

Merryn's confidence drained away as the Fairy soldiers advanced. She slumped onto the rocky outcrop. What would she do if the sporran refused to open? But it not only opened, it tipped the contents into her lap. As the crystals tumbled out, their light shone far into the night. Hamish dashed to pick up the yellow crystal. Defiantly he held it as high as he could. Merryn held up the pink one. The lines of light formed themselves into a figure of eight. They passed through the purple crystal on Merryn's lap, and a feeling of hope flowed with them. And when she saw that the Fairy woman had not noticed the crystals, her confidence returned.

'I see no periwinkle,' said the Fairy woman. 'There are but eighty. You lied to me.'

'My sister doesn't lie,' Hamish shouted, 'and neither do I. The periwinkle isn't missing at all. It's in the bowl with all the others."

'Take care, mortal boy. You anger me. If you do not lie, then you miscounted.' She pointed to the tape measure. 'I'll take that too. It will come in useful for measuring the cotton.'

Merryn hesitated. She wanted to refuse, to say that it belonged to Aunt Aggie and that she'd be in trouble if she didn't return it. But the Fairy woman held out her hand.

'I will take the tape measure,' she repeated.

Reluctantly Merryn handed it over. Without a word of thanks the Fairy woman placed it on the velvet cushion alongside the ball of thread and the necklace of sea-beans and hag-stones.

'Now I will take the crystals!' She held out her hand and laughed, and all around her the sound of Fairy laughter filled the air.

'Foolish child, you thought I had not noticed them. You should have known that I too have The Gift, for did I not see the horse, the necklace and the sporran? Give the crystals to me, for they are far too powerful for the likes of you. Give them to me now and I will forget the last periwinkle.'

Hamish hid the yellow crystal behind his back. Merryn's fist closed over the pink one. Kester lowered his head and covered the purple one with his nose, and the figure of eight didn't falter.

'No,' said Merryn. 'I will not give them to you.'

The Fairy soldiers advanced. Now they stood shoulder to shoulder with scarce a gap between them.

'How dare you refuse?' demanded the Fairy woman. 'Give the crystals to me, all three of them, now.'

'No,' Merryn said again. Suddenly her head filled with words, words that rushed out of her mouth like a river in flood.

'I will not give the crystals to you because they are not mine to give. It is unjust of you to ask, for we made a bargain. We have kept our part and I have been honest. You have tried to trick us at every turn. You took the silver bell. You took the garland of moon daisies. You took the necklace of sea-beans and hag-stones. You took the ball of thread and my Aunt Aggie's tape measure, and I will have to answer for their loss. And whatever you say, we did put eighty-one yellow periwinkles in the paper bag.'

The Fairy woman folded her arms and stared hard into Merryn's eyes. 'You are wrong,' she said. 'I will tell you for the last time, you have brought only eighty periwinkles. I will take the crystals to make up for the loss.'

Chapter 27

Merryn knew that the Fairy woman was trying to trick her. She had deliberately miscounted the periwinkles so that she could demand to see inside the sporran. Now she was threatening to take the crystals too. Merryn looked at Kester with tears in her eyes. He gave the softest of whinnies, nudged her with his nose and tossed his head in the direction of the silver bowl. Of course, why hadn't she thought of it before?

'If you will not count the periwinkles again, I will count them for you. I will prove that there are eighty-one. I will not only stake my life on it, I will stake the life of my brother and of Kester, the horse.'

A great muttering rose from mound. The Fairy soldiers began to thump the ground with the base of their spears.

The witch screamed. 'Don't let her. Don't let her.'

The Fairy woman turned and walked around the mound. The witch went on screaming. The voices from inside the hill grew louder. The spears of the Fairy soldiers thumped so hard that the mound vibrated to their rhythm.

Merryn took out the crystal pendulum and held it, suspended, in front of her. Kester gave the softest of whinnies. He was the only one who had noticed it. Many minutes passed before the Fairy woman came again to stand in front of them.

'I have tested your endurance to the limit,' she said. 'You have not veered from the truth and you have shown great courage. It is as you say. You do not need to count the periwinkles again. Nine times nine I asked of you, and nine times nine there are. But remember this, to doubt the word of a Fairy is foolhardy, and to refuse a request from a Fairy is reckless in the extreme. Others would have punished you severely for such defiance.'

She looked towards Kester and her gaze rested on the necklace. 'I would have given much to own it,' she said, 'the crystals too. I covet them and would have won them from anyone less determined than you. Yet I sense that your need is greater than mine, and I understand the importance of your Quest. If you succeed the horse will not be the only one to benefit. You intrigue me mortal child. You are but half grown and yet your bravery exceeds that of the adult mortals of today. There is something of the past in your manner. Tell me, were you always so? Or was all this for love of the horse? Speak freely, child. I will not test you again. Tell me what is in your heart.'

Merryn heard a different note in the Fairy woman's voice. There was a hint of kindness that seemed genuine. Even so, she found it difficult to trust one who had repeatedly tried to get the better of her. The crystal pendulum was still swinging, sending its light far beyond Fang an t-Sithein; but the Fairy woman had not seen it. She could not be trusted. As Merryn wondered how to reply, the Fairy woman stepped closer. Her eyes narrowed as if she was trying to see something that wasn't quite there.

'Ah!' she said as she focussed on the crystal pendulum. 'Now I see the source of your power. With that in your possession, you could not fail to win me over. It is of great importance. You must guard it well.'

A wave of relief surged through Merryn. The Fairy woman had changed her mind. She could see the pendulum. She was no longer a threat. Kester's soft muzzle snuffled at Merryn's fingertips and she knew that he was encouraging her to speak.

No longer relying on help from Kester's Book, her own words tumbled out in a rush. 'When I heard the horse calling for help I had to find him, and once I'd found him I had to rescue him. I was scared, especially when the witch arrived. But I couldn't stop, and I won't stop until he's free.' She faltered and pointed at the witch. 'As for her, I don't know what will happen. All I know is that I have to stop her.'

Forcing her thoughts away from the danger that lay ahead, she turned back to the Fairy woman. 'Coming to Fang an t-Sithein for the heart-stone was the second task. I don't know what to do with it, but I am sure it will be needed for the next challenge.' She ran her hand down Kester's neck and rested her cheek against his. 'I don't know how many challenges are left, but however many there are, I'll face them all.'

'I do not doubt it,' said the Fairy woman. She turned to Hamish. 'Tell me, where do you fit into this? You are younger than your sister and you do not have The Gift. I can smell your fear, and yet you too stand your ground. Why did you allow yourself to become involved?'

'I couldn't let Merryn do it by herself,' said Hamish. 'She's my sister and she needed me. I promised to help, and once I'd promised, I had to keep on helping. I was scared. I'm still scared. I'm scared stiff but I won't let it stop me. The witch called me a wimp. I'll show her that I'm not and we'll win in the end.'

'If the will to win is all that is needed,' said the Fairy woman, 'then success will be yours. But do not underestimate the power of that particular witch. I do not understand her mission, but I believe she will fight until her dying breath.'

'I know,' said Merryn, 'but we won't give in.'

'That I believe,' said the Fairy woman, 'but I foresee great battles ahead. There is more at stake than saving the life of a horse. The witch who sits on yonder boulder is only one of many evil creatures who strive to dominate the world.'

Hamish shuddered and drew even closer to Merryn.

'But do not lose heart,' the Fairy woman said to him. 'Your support for your sister will be remembered. The witch is wrong. You have shown great courage. You are not a wimp.'

She smiled at Merryn. 'You were chosen to save the horse, and if you succeed you will have played a vital part in the fight for all that is good and true. I tested you sorely because I had to know if you were worthy of the heart-stone. Had you cowered before me, had you buckled to my will, had you tried to lie and cheat, I could not have loaned it to you. It will only work for those who show honesty, courage, loyalty and determination. You have those qualities in abundance. For those reasons, I will accept the periwinkles and I will...'

'I warned you,' yelled the witch as she rose into the air and hovered high above Fang an t-Sithein. 'I warned you not to accept. From this day forward we are at war. When I have eliminated the three who stand before you, I will eliminate you and your people.'

The Fairy soldiers turned towards the witch. They raised their bows and sent a volley of fiery darts winging towards her.

'Fire away!' she shouted. 'I am invincible. Your darts cannot touch me.' She hooted with laughter as she dodged dart after dart, but when one of them caught the twigs at the end of the broomstick, her laughter turned to yells of rage. The twigs burst into flame. A cheer rose from the Fairy soldiers as the witch on her burning broomstick turned and headed towards the loch.

'Faster,' screamed the witch, 'into the loch. Put out the fire.' As the broomstick rushed through the air, the breeze fanned the flames. They spread until all the twigs were alight. By the time the broomstick plunged into the water, most of them had turned to ash. The witch, grinding her teeth and cursing, struggled to her feet and waded to the shore. Dripping wet and festooned with waterweeds, she climbed onto what remained of the broomstick and ordered it to fly. Without the birch twigs it was no longer balanced. It dipped forwards at such a sharp angle that the tip of the shaft buried itself in the soft earth.

'You stupid, useless thing,' she fumed. Seething with anger she used all her strength to keep the broomstick level, but it still couldn't fly. Soaked from her dunking in the loch, and bewildered by yet another failure, she made her weary way back to the souterrain.

Once again she would have to mend the broomstick. A few twigs still lay on the floor, but if there weren't enough she would have to go out for more. She groaned at the prospect, for she was exhausted, and she had plans for the rest of the day. She had to make a spell that was more powerful than any she had ever made before. She had to make a spell that would destroy the horse and those interfering children once and for all.

Chapter 28

The witch's screams died away, but her threats hung in the air. The Fairy woman covered her face with her hands. All around the mound a deathly silence fell.

Hamish clutched Merryn's hand. 'It's our fault,' he whispered. 'The witch only came because she followed us. If I'd known we were going to start a war I wouldn't have come.'

'Neither would I,' said Merryn. She looked from Kester to the Fairy woman and she raised her hands in despair. 'Is there nothing I can say, nothing we can do to help?'

Kester stood with his head bowed as if he too felt the burden of blame.

At last, the Fairy woman uncovered her eyes. 'You have your own Quest to follow,' she said. 'There is nothing for you here. The greatest help you can give is to defeat the witch. Concentrate on that and leave us to prepare ourselves for war.'

She stood on top of the mound and called out in a voice as loud and clear as a bell. 'Come, my people. Come, one and all.'

At her words, a host of Fairy Folk emerged from the hill. They came in one's and two's, in family groups, fathers with toddlers on their shoulders, mothers with babes in their arms, children of all sizes, old people walking hesitantly, and lastly, the lame, leaning on sticks and crutches. Every face was pale and grave and not one of them uttered so much as a whisper.

'I had no idea,' Merryn choked on a sob. Tears flowed down her cheeks. She tried to brush them away, but still they fell. 'There are so many of you, and if the witch harms you, it will be my fault.'

The Fairy woman, obviously deep in thought, placed her palms together. 'You are not to blame,' she said. 'You are on the side of all that is honest and true. You have jolted me out of my complacency. I must urge my people to fight for what, in our hearts, we know to be right.'

Turning to the silent crowd, she spoke out. 'We have worked hard and we have been rewarded with lives of comfort and plenty. We have revelled in feasting, in music and dancing, but we have neglected all that occurs beyond our happy domain.'

She pointed to the tumble of stones surrounding Fang an t-Sithein. 'Why! We have even allowed our boundary wall to go unrepaired. It is time for change. We must not let the evil ones spread their influence across the earth. We must rise up and fight. Go now and consider everything I have said. Tonight we will sit together and prepare a plan of action. In the meantime, I must conclude my business with these brave mortal children.'

Raising her arm she faced the gap in the stone wall. Slowly she turned full circle, and as her finger pointed at the Fairy Folk, each and every one of them slipped silently into the earth. When they had all disappeared she sank down on the rocky outcrop and motioned to Merryn and Hamish to sit down beside her.

'There are trying times ahead for us all,' she said, 'but I have accepted the bell, the garland, the necklace and the periwinkles. Now it is for me to uphold the

174

bargain. But before I put the heart-stone in your hand, there are questions that must be answered.

Merryn drew in her breath and raised her eyes to the sky. Surely they had done enough. Just when she thought they'd won the heart-stone the Fairy woman was asking for something else. She gripped Hamish by the arm, and hoped beyond hope that she would be able to answer the questions.

'How came you by the necklace of sea-beans and hag-stones?'

Merryn relaxed and let go of Hamish's arm. If all the questions were as easy as this, she would have nothing to fear. 'I found it inside a wooden box in my Aunt Aggie's cottage.'

The Fairy woman accepted the answer and followed it with another question. 'And what do you know of its origin?'

'I know that it was made to protect my great-great-great-great-grandmother from witchcraft and that a Selkie helped her to make it.'

'Ah!' The Fairy woman gave a faint smile. 'That would certainly explain its magical qualities. But do you know anything about the Selkie?'

'I do,' she said. 'His name is Roane. I have spoken with him and he told me why the necklace was made.'

The Fairy woman nodded approvingly. 'It is as I thought. Tell me, was it the same Roane who gave the crystal pendulum into your keeping?'

Merryn nodded. Hamish, who had never believed Merryn's account of meeting the Selkie, looked from one to the other with an expression of total bewilderment.

'And now,' said the Fairy woman. 'I will tell you something. Your great-great-great-great-grandmother was Merryn MacQueen.'

Merryn's eyes grew wide with surprise. 'It was! But how could you know that?'

'I knew of the service she did for Roane. All the Fairy Folk knew and respected her for it. She was renowned for her wisdom. Had I realised that you were descended from Merryn MacQueen, I would not have tested you so sorely. What is your name child?'

'Merryn MacQueen.'

The Fairy woman laughed out loud. 'I should have known, for when I look at you through eyes of friendship I see the resemblance. You not only inherited The Gift, you inherited her colouring as well. Now that I know who you are, I am happy to lend the heart-stone.'

'Yes!' Hamish leapt to his feet and cheered. 'We've done it!'

The Fairy woman laughed. 'I understand your triumph,' she said, 'but sit down again. Before I give it to you, there are things you need to know. You must use it for no purpose other than that which your challenge requires. When it has fulfilled its task, it will return to me of its own accord. So do not be concerned when it disappears.'

A frown crossed her face as she nodded towards the witch. 'Most importantly, do not let it fall into her hands. If she takes possession of it, we will lose the war before it has even begun.'

Out of her apron pocket she pulled a bag of purple silk. It dangled from her finger on black, tasselled threads. 'The heart-stone is inside, but you must not take it out until the moment it is needed.'

Merryn opened her mouth to protest, but the Fairy woman placed a finger to her lips. 'You must trust me,' she said. 'You have my word of honour that the heart-stone is inside. I will not try to trick you again.'

She placed the bag in Merryn's hand. 'For now it slumbers, but when the time is right it will awake and enter into the spirit of your Quest. All it asks is that you believe implicitly in its power. If your faith falters, it will be useless. Remember too, that the loan is for two nights only, this night and one night more. That was the bargain we struck and it is not in my power to change it. So make haste, and do whatever it is that you have to do.'

She rose to her feet and nodded approvingly. 'You have faced up to me and emerged with honour. Few, if any, could do as well as you have done. Now you must leave Fang an t-Sithein, for I have serious business to attend to. It concerns the witch who is now my enemy as well as yours. We share a common cause. So one day our paths may cross again.'

She took a step towards Kester. This time he did not flinch. He lowered his head and allowed her to stroke the length of his nose. She whispered something in his ear, something Merryn was unable to hear. He gave a gentle whinny and tossed his head as if in reply.

The Fairy woman turned away, paused, and raised her hand. 'Tell no-one what has passed between us. Do not falter in your Quest, and may courage go with you.'

Merryn, remembering the instructions from Kester's Book, bowed her head and once again lapsed into the strange formal language. 'We are honoured to have made your acquaintance and we are eternally grateful for the loan of the heart-stone. Now we bid you farewell.'

When she raised her head, the Fairy woman had gone. The heart-stone in its silken bag was safe inside the sporran. A delighted smile settled on her face. 'We did it,' she said to Hamish. 'We really did it.'

As they mounted Kester and prepared to leave Fang an t-Sithein, her smile faded. Somewhere out there the witch was waiting – waiting to stop them, waiting to burst the bubble, waiting to steal the heart-stone, waiting to do her worst.

Chapter 29

A faint glow marked the eastern horizon, but as they sped along the sands of Gott Bay the sky grew dark. It was impossible to know just when the sun would rise. Black billowing clouds formed above the sea. Beneath them the sky was streaked with curtains of rain. There was a flash followed by the sound of distant thunder. Seconds later, another streak of lightning lit the sky.

The thunder rumbled closer. Kester lowered his head and galloped for all he was worth. They travelled through heavy rain, and all the time, the storm was moving closer and closer. Flashes and rumbles came together. The storm in all its fury was directly above their heads. Blinding lightning zigzagged from sky to sea. Thunder clapped so loudly that Merryn was desperate to cover her ears, but she daren't let go of Kester's mane.

Hamish tightened his arms about Merryn's waist. He screamed as lightning struck a rock that lay in front of them. Kester galloped round it, but he could not outrun the storm. For many minutes it flashed and crashed on every side. And it was not until they had passed through the eye of it, that he slowed, first to a canter and then to a trot.

'I thought the witch had sent it,' said Hamish, 'but she didn't. It was a real storm. Look, we're wet through. If the witch had caused it, the bubble would have kept us dry.'

'I know,' said Merryn, 'but even if she didn't send it, she'll still try to stop us. She's sure to be lying in wait somewhere.'

'Maybe she isn't,' said Hamish hopefully. 'Maybe she drowned in the loch, or maybe her broomstick was burnt so badly that she can't fly anymore.'

'You wish!' said Merryn. 'But I don't think we'll get back without seeing her again. Hurry, Kester, hurry.'

Kester began to gallop again. The rain kept on falling but the sound of the storm lay behind them and nothing else stood in their way. The witch did not re-appear. They reached the post with time to spare. They slipped from Kester's back and the three of them stood with their heads together. Kester's flanks were heaving after so much effort, but he nuzzled them both and gradually his breathing slowed to normal.

'I don't want to leave you,' said Merryn as she stroked the length of his nose. 'I don't know what our next task will be, but I won't let you down. I promise.'

'Neither will I,' added Hamish. 'It can't be worse than facing the Fairy woman and all those soldiers.' He looked uncertainly at Merryn. 'It can't, can it?'

Merryn shrugged. 'I hope not. We've no way of telling. I just hope that whatever it is, it'll be the last one.'

With soft words of encouragement she slipped the necklace from Kester's neck onto her own. Once again the dark murky colours swirled around them. She covered her ears to block out the discordant sounds. She tried not to breathe in the filthy vapour but she couldn't turn away until Kester had disappeared. It was horrible knowing that he was trapped again, but it seemed to be the safest place for him during the hours of daylight. And he only had to wait until midnight before she released him once more.

'I wonder,' she said to Hamish, 'where the witch goes during the day. She must be hiding somewhere because we only ever see her when it's dark. I wish we knew.'

'Yes!' said Hamish, 'then we could take her by surprise. We could ambush her, steal her broomstick and burn her house down. That's what we can do today. We can go out and find her hiding place.'

A thoughtful frown settled on Merryn's face. 'Let's not be too hasty,' she said. 'It's bound to be dangerous. We'd best see what Kester's Book has to say. For now, we have to think about Aunt Aggie and what she'll say if she sees the state we're in.'

Although the storm had passed and the rain had thinned to a fine drizzle every stitch of their clothing was dripping. They jogged their way back to the cottage only to find that their ordeal wasn't over. The sight that met Merryn brought her to a sudden stop. It wasn't as bad as facing the witch, but it was bad enough. She clapped one hand over her mouth and clutched Hamish with the other.

'Oh! Crumbs,' Hamish groaned, 'now we're for it.'

Aunt Aggie, with her nightdress trailing beneath her oilskin coat, was hammering on Donald's door. Beyond her, the tent, torn from two of its pegs, was flapping wildly. Sleeping bags and pyjamas were strewn across the grass. Donald appeared. He was pulling on a coat over his striped pyjamas. Aunt Aggie was waving her arms about as if she was trying to tell him something.

He put his hand on her shoulder. It looked as if he was trying to calm her.

'Look,' he said as they drew near the gate. 'Wherever they've been they're back. They're safe. Let's get indoors. We can clear up the mess later.'

Aunt Aggie turned and looked at them. Her face was white and drawn. She grabbed the doorframe to steady herself. 'You'll be the death of me,' she gasped. 'I'll...'

'Not now,' said Donald as he helped her back to her cottage. 'We'll have a cup of tea. Then we can talk about what happened. You two get out of those wet clothes while I stoke up the fire and put the kettle on.'

Too shocked to speak, they made their way upstairs. Merryn couldn't forget the look on Aunt Aggie's face. However mean she was, she obviously cared about them. Overwhelmed with guilt she wondered how to put things right. But what could she do? Stopping the Quest wouldn't help. The witch would still seek them out, and if she tried to burn the cottage again she might succeed. That really would give Aunt Aggie something to be upset about.

Hamish, his hair still wet, but in dry clothes, came into her room. He was as pale as Aunt Aggie. Merryn could find no words to reassure him. She was being torn apart. She couldn't abandon Kester. She had to save all three of them from the witch. But it was impossible to do any of these things without upsetting Aunt Aggie.

'We'd better go down,' she whispered, 'but we'll have to be careful what we say. We went for a walk, that's all. Leave the talking to me.'

Feeling sick with apprehension she led him downstairs. Aunt Aggie was sitting by the fire; her head thrown back against a cushion. Donald had his back to them. He turned and shook his head as if he couldn't believe their stupidity. For ages no-one said a word.

Aunt Aggie finally broke the silence, her voice unsteady, words faltering.

'What...what were you doing? Going out in a thunderstorm was...was madness.'

Hamish, obviously forgetting Merryn's instructions looked down at his feet. 'It wasn't raining when we went out,' he mumbled.

Aunt Aggie's head jerked up. Her shock seemed to have subsided and she blazed with anger. 'But the storm started hours ago. You must have gone out in the middle of the night.'

'I'm not sure what time it was,' said Merryn. 'We couldn't sleep. It got really hot and we needed some fresh air. We didn't mean to...'

Hamish butted in. Nerves making his words run away with him. 'I just wanted to see the sea. It's exciting when it's rough. You should have seen the waves. They were crashing and sending spray right up into the air. It was...' Responding to a nudge from Merryn he faltered and hung his head. 'I suppose I'm going to get all the blame.'

'I'm blaming you both,' snapped Aunt Aggie, 'and I'll tell you this. Any more stunts like that and I'll put you on the next plane. And this time I mean it.'

'You can't,' said Hamish. 'Mum and dad are busy. There's nowhere for us to go.'

'I don't care how busy they are,' said Aunt Aggie, 'and don't try to tell me what to do. Plans will have to be changed. From now on you do as you're told. There'll be no more sleeping in the tent. You'll go to your rooms immediately after supper and you'll stay there until I call you for breakfast.'

Merryn and Hamish gasped. 'But,' they said together.

Donald gave them a warning look. 'That seems fair to me,' he said. 'I don't think you realise the danger you were in. On a low-lying island like Tiree, you could have been struck by lightning. And even if there wasn't a storm, you shouldn't be wandering around at night. If something happened to you, we wouldn't know where to find you.'

'Wandering around at night,' Aunt Aggie exclaimed. 'They'll not be wandering around in the daytime either. From now on they don't set foot outside the garden without me.'

Chapter 30

Merryn and Hamish burst into tears and clung to one another. It was unfair. If Aunt Aggie had her way it would be the end of the Quest. Kester would stay in the fencepost for ever, and the witch would go on with her horrible magic. They could do nothing to explain. Begging and pleading would make no impression on Aunt Aggie. The crying went on for a long time. When the tears eventually subsided, Hamish put his head in his hands and groaned. Merryn chewed her knuckles anxiously as she tried to figure a way out of Aunt Aggie's new rules. Tonight they had to use the heart-stone. Whatever Aunt Aggie said, and however she tried to stop them, they couldn't give up now.

Donald left. Aunt Aggie ran her fingers through her hair and shook her head. 'When I agreed to let you stay,' she said. 'I didn't expect this. Get out of my sight, go to bed, the pair of you. I'll have more to say in the morning.'

Feeling guilty, but not knowing what to say, Merryn took Hamish by the arm and left the room.

'What are we going to do?' Hamish started to cry all over again. 'We can't let Kester down, but we can't upset Aunt Aggie again. She looked awful. I thought she was going to fall down and die.'

'So did I,' said Merryn, 'but I think she'll be OK now and we'd better try to sleep. We can make plans in the morning.'

Breakfast time was far worse than usual. Aunt Aggie seemed too exhausted to say anything. She just sent them to their rooms with instructions not to show their faces until lunch was ready.

Back upstairs, Merryn turned to Hamish. 'I've made a decision,' she said. 'I've got to do whatever Kester's Book tells me, but you're not coming.'

'I jolly well am,' he protested. 'We're in this together, right to the very end.'

'It's not that I don't want you,' she sighed. 'I just think one of us should stay here in case Aunt Aggie wakes up and misses us. I'd do it myself, only I can't because I'm the one with the necklace.'

As she spoke, Kester's Book leapt out of the sporran. Words appeared rapidly, words that disagreed with her decision.

Tonight, whatever the risk,
both of you are needed at the Ringing Stone.
You did extremely well at Fang an t-Sithein.
You stood your ground
and you have the heart-stone.
I could not have asked more of you.

'See,' said Hamish triumphantly. 'I've got to go and you can't stop me.'

Merryn couldn't argue with Kester's book. 'You win,' she said, 'but I don't know how we're going to get out without Aunt Aggie stopping us.'

'I bet she snores. I'll listen from the stairs,' said Hamish, 'and when we're sure she's asleep we can sneak out. If she wakes up we'll just have to run.'

'I suppose so,' said Merryn, 'although she'll be in a terrible state by the time we get back. But look, there's more writing.'

Even now, the witch is making new
and powerful spells.
You must work together to turn them aside.
Hamish, you must keep Kester calm.
If you fail, the whole task will be in jeopardy.
Merryn, success depends
on you memorising the instructions.

Hamish scowled. 'I still don't see why you get the best bits. Just because you're older than...'

'Not that again,' Merryn interrupted. 'It's not my fault that I was born before you. If I could swap with you I would, but I can't so there's no point in arguing. I couldn't have managed without you at Fang an t-Sithein. You were really brave, and I need you to be brave again tonight.'

She handed him one of the old books from the chest in the cubbyhole. 'Here, see what you can find out about the Ringing Stone. And when it stops raining you can clear up the tent. Now leave me alone while I find out what I have to do.'

'If you think I'm doing all the boring stuff, you can think again.' Hamish stuck out his bottom lip and glowered. 'I'm staying here. I want to know what the book says. Then I can remind you if you forget.'

'I don't intend to forget,' she said, 'but I suppose it's not a bad idea.'

She turned back to Kester's Book as more words appeared.

Tonight you will face
the greatest challenge so far.
If you succeed the Quest will be over
and you will be freed from your promises.

'Yes!' She grinned at Hamish. 'This is it, the last task!'

'It might not be,' said Hamish, 'look, it's still writing.'

However, if you fail,
there will be even harder challenges ahead.

Her grin disappeared. A feeling of hopelessness washed over her. The greatest challenge so far didn't bear thinking about. For the briefest of moments she wished they could give up. But Kester's frantic neigh filled her head and pushed the negative thought away.

'So,' she said, 'there's no question of failing. We've got to succeed, then Kester will be free, and so will we.'

'And the witch?' asked Hamish. 'What do you think will happen to her?'

Merryn frowned. 'I don't know. It doesn't say.'

She turned back to the book and went through the instructions. They were long and complicated. She read them over and over. She did a dummy run, pretending that the chair was the Ringing Stone. She paced round it as she tried to fix the movements in her head. When she was sure she knew exactly what to do, she picked up the old book.

'The Ringing Stone is a big rock,' she said, 'and it's covered with little hollows called cup marks. They were made in the Stone Age and I think they may be important.' She raised her voice. 'Are you listening?'

Hamish grunted. 'No. I've changed my mind. I don't need to know about the stone. All I have to do is look after Kester. So don't bother telling me.'

Merryn thumbed through the book. 'You'll be interested in this though. You wanted to find the witch's hiding place and I think this might be it. There's a thing called a souterrain. It's an underground room where people used to hide from invaders in days gone by. Maybe that's where she goes during the daytime.'

'It's no use telling me,' he grumbled. 'We can't go and look for it now.'

After she'd mended her broomstick, the witch started the real business of the day. She searched through her book of spells and laughed aloud when she found what she was seeking. It meant leaving the souterrain in daylight. That was something she dreaded, but she had no choice. She filled her cauldron with water, herbs and waterweeds. From her store she took the tooth of a water horse and the claw of a mountain dragon. She cut her black toenails, her long fingernails and a length of her greasy hair. She dropped them all into the cauldron and stirred until the mixture boiled.

'I will burst the bubble,' she said. 'I will snatch the heart-stone. I will flatten Fang an t-Sithein. I will wipe out the Fairy Folk. I will eliminate the girl and her brother. I will make Kester watch them suffer, and then I will end his life for ever.'

She rubbed her hands together gleefully. 'I will gatecrash the Festival of Malevolent Witches. I will hold up Kester's sporran and every single witch will cheer. The Grand High Witch will apologise for banishing me. I will keep the heart-stone for myself and I will use it against anyone who stands in my way.'

She cleared her throat, hawked up a gobbet of phlegm and spat it into the furiously bubbling liquid. Chanting strings of evil words, she stirred and stirred until the mixture blended into a sticky, black mass. She leaned over the cauldron, inhaling deeply. The smell of death that filled her nostrils brought a smile of satisfaction to her wrinkled face.

Finally, she took a bundle of arrows and dipped them into the stinking potion. She turned them round and round until they were thoroughly coated with black magic. Not until they were tied in a bundle did she lie down to rest.

For Hamish and Merryn, banned from setting foot outside the garden, time passed slowly. They tidied up the mess made by the storm, hung the wet things up to dry and pegged the tent back into place. They lay on the bed, dozing a little, looking at books and waiting for the day to end. Aunt Aggie kept her word and sent them back upstairs as soon as supper was over.

Merryn wanted to sleep, but she couldn't even close her eyes. She was too guilty about disobeying Aunt Aggie, and too anxious about the task that lay ahead.

At eight o'clock, Aunt Aggie came upstairs. 'Bed,' she ordered. 'There'll be no more talking tonight.'

Merryn wanted to say she was sorry, but the words stuck in her throat. She couldn't apologise when she knew they were about to break the rules again.

'I don't trust you,' said Aunt Aggie, 'So I've locked the doors. There'll be no sneaking out tonight.'

She jangled a bunch of keys as she spoke. 'I'm going to bed and I'd better not hear a sound before breakfast.'

Hamish stared at Merryn in shocked disbelief. Her eyes filled with tears of frustration as Aunt Aggie launched into another tirade.

'Make no mistake, she snapped. 'One more stunt like the last and you're leaving. I've reached the end of my tether. Someone will have to meet you and I don't care who it is.'

Hamish stomped past Aunt Aggie, went to his room, and slammed the door.

'I thought a girl would have more sense,' said Aunt Aggie to Merryn, 'but I was wrong. I'm at my wits end with both of you. Now I'm away down to my bed and I'll leave my bedroom door open. So if you start sneaking about, I'll hear you.'

With one last frown at Merryn, she left the room and closed the door firmly behind her.

Chapter 31

Would all their plans come to nothing? Shocked by Aunt Aggie's last outburst, Merryn couldn't sit still. She walked round the room. She threw herself on the bed. She went to the window and looked out. A full moon shone from a cloudless sky. It was a perfect night for ending the Quest. But how could they get out of the cottage?

The doors were locked. Aunt Aggie's bedroom was at the bottom of the stairs. They couldn't sneak past her open door to reach a downstairs window without waking her. The bedroom windows set into the roof were too high. The cubbyhole window, on the gable end was too small.

Or was it? Squeezing through and dropping onto the porch roof seemed to be the only possible way out. It wouldn't be easy. It might even be dangerous. The flat roof might not bear their weight. From the roof to the ground was still a long drop, and although a wheelie bin stood alongside, they might not be able to reach it. And even if they got out, they wouldn't be able to get back in.

Before she had time to check, Hamish came in on tiptoe. 'Aunt Aggie's snoring,' he whispered, 'and I don't care what she said. We've got to get out. We'll have to sneak downstairs and get out of a window.'

'No,' she said. 'I have a better idea.'

With her finger to her lips she led him behind the wardrobe, through the curtain and into the cubbyhole.

'You rotten thing,' he protested as he looked round. 'I thought we were sharing everything. You've been hiding this all along. It's not fair.'

'Never mind that now,' she hissed. 'We've got to be quiet.'

She handed him the key. 'Lock the door and put the key in your pocket. I'll open the window, and if I can get through we'll be fine. We're above the porch roof and once I reach it I'll get to the ground, even if I have to jump.'

She pushed open the window and looked apprehensively at the narrow space. It was going to be a very tight squeeze. Peeling off her fleece, she stood on the windowsill and pushed her legs through the gap. She wriggled and squirmed, and only got her hips through by turning sideways. Now she was stuck. Her head and shoulders were still inside the room. She twisted and turned, until, like a cork popping from a bottle, she shot through and landed on the porch roof with a clatter.

Hamish, skinnier and smaller, was through in seconds. He helped her to her feet, and they stood, hardly daring to breath, listening for sounds of Aunt Aggie stirring. All they heard was snoring. Merryn put on her fleece, lowered herself onto the wheelie bin and jumped to the ground. Hamish followed. Not daring to look back, they ran until the cottage was far behind them.

Slowing to a jog, Merryn pushed worries about Aunt Aggie to the back of her mind. Now she must concentrate on facing the witch. Any minute now, she expected her to appear, and there, ahead of them, was proof that she'd already been at work. The track was a mass of stones, each one pointing upwards, each one with a tip as sharp as the point of a dagger.

Hamish gulped and came to a sudden stop. 'We can't cross those. They'll burst the bubble. They'll cut it to ribbons.'

'Then we'll walk round them,' said Merryn. 'That should be easy enough.'

'Oh! No it isn't,' screeched the witch as she swooped towards them.

The witch was right. When they veered to the left the stones moved with them. When they turned to the right, the same thing happened. As Hamish whirled round, the stones gathered in a circle. Each time they advanced, the jagged points pushed into the bubble and they had to retreat for fear of it bursting.

The witch hovered on her broomstick. She brought her face close to the bubble. Baring her teeth and grinning, she waved a bundle of black-tipped arrows.

'Now I've got you,' she snarled. 'These will burst your beastly bubble.' She swung away on the broomstick, held up her first arrow and made ready to shoot.

'Do something,' Hamish yelled. 'Stop her.'

Merryn's brain seemed to freeze, but a sudden rush of adrenalin spurred her into action. She tried to pull out the crystal pendulum, but its chain tangled with the sea-bean and hag-stone necklace. By the time she'd freed it, the witch had sent an arrow winging towards them. Unlike every other missile the witch had sent, it didn't bounce off the bubble. It didn't fall to the ground. Merryn gasped as its tip lodged in the skin of the bubble. It hung there, wobbling, but it didn't break through.

'Get the crystals,' she shouted, 'but don't touch the heart-stone.'

The sporran opened and Hamish took out the crystals. As the figure of eight began to swirl round the inside of the bubble, the witch sent a second arrow. It drove more deeply into the bubble. There was a sudden hissing sound like that made by air when it leaks out of a balloon.

'She's done it,' Hamish screamed. 'She's burst our bubble.'

As air escaped through the hole made by the arrow, the hissing grew louder. The punctured side of the bubble began to collapse.

'Hit it with your crystal,' Merryn shouted. 'Quick.'

Hamish thrust the yellow crystal at the hole. The air kept on hissing. The bubble kept on collapsing.

'It's not working,' he yelled.

'Try the purple one,' Merryn shouted, 'that's the most powerful.'

Hamish hit the hole with the purple crystal. Immediately, the arrow shot backwards and fell to the ground. The hissing stopped, but the bubble was badly dented, and it didn't regain its shape. Merryn now had the pendulum in her hand. She dangled it from its golden chain. It wobbled and dithered, but her hand shook so much that it failed to find a rhythm.

The witch, zooming round on her broomstick, fired a third arrow. A bevy of others followed in quick succession. Every one of them penetrated the bubble. Hamish swung his arm from side to side hitting the arrow tips with the purple crystal. As the arrows fell away, the punctures seemed to heal, but too much air had been lost.

The bubble collapsed, leaving them inside a space so small that they had to fall to their knees and lower their heads. Merryn, forgetting everything except her brother and the danger, flung her arms round him and held him tight.

The witch flew down. She leapt off her broomstick and leered at them. 'Now I have you, you interfering brats.'

'Mum,' Hamish sobbed as he buried his face in Merryn's fleece. 'I want my mum.'

The witch laughed her hideous laugh. 'Not just a wimp,' she sneered, 'a cry baby too. I'll give you something to cry about.' She brandished her last three arrows. 'See these? There's one for each of you and one for the horse. Go now and release him. Then I will put an end to you all.'

Merryn's head filled with voices.

First to speak was the Fairy woman. 'Do not falter in your Quest, and may courage go with you.'

Next came Roane's words. 'Be brave and face whatever lies ahead.'

Lastly, there came a voice that she had never heard before. It spoke the words from Kester's Book. Over and over again it said, 'Stand your ground. Stand your ground. Stand your ground.'

She let go of Hamish and held the pendulum as steadily as her shaking hands allowed. Slowly it began to describe a circle. Gathering momentum, it flew faster and faster. Its light grew brighter and brighter. The skin of the bubble began to quiver.

'It's working,' she cried. 'Hamish, look. It's working.'

The bubble grew larger. Soon they were able to stand up and lift their heads.

The witch hopped up and down. Holding the arrows like spears, she thrust them towards Merryn. As she touched the bubble, the black tips ignited, flames ran back up the shafts and burned her hands. Screaming, she dropped them, lunged forwards and pushed her shoulder against the growing bubble. She grabbed her broomstick and stooped to retrieve the arrows that had fallen earlier. As she picked them up, they too burst into flame.

Still holding the crystal pendulum, Merryn faced the witch. The bubble grew larger than ever before. It pushed the witch farther and farther away until, with an ear-splitting howl, she mounted her broomstick and headed towards the wooden post.

Hamish grabbed Merryn's hand. 'You did it,' he cheered. 'She's gone, and look, her horrible spiky rocks have gone as well.'

Merryn nodded. 'Don't be fooled though. She hasn't given up. She'll try something else. I know she will. Come on, we've got to run, Kester's waiting.'

The witch was waiting too. She was hovering high above Kester's post and she was roaring with hideous laughter. Eager to release Kester, Merryn threw the necklace over the post. Nothing happened. There were neither lights, nor sound, nor movement. The witch had indeed tried something else. She had trapped Kester in another spell.

Chapter 32

Kester was locked inside the post and the necklace had failed to release him. Merryn tried again. She held her breath as the sea-bean and hag-stone necklace dropped over his wooden head. Still nothing happened.

Hamish stepped back in shock. 'We're stumped,' he said.

'Don't say that,' Merryn snapped. 'We can't be. We've got to find a way.'

Once again she pulled out the crystal pendulum. It had already broken some of the witch's spells. Hoping desperately that it would break this one too, she suspended it above the post.

'Come on, come on,' she urged.

Slowly the pendulum began to swing. The witch zoomed down and peered into the bubble. She clawed at it with what was left of her fingernails. The pendulum swung faster. The post pulsed and throbbed as wave after wave of light passed into it. Finally, there was a blinding flash and the light was gone.

'No!' Hamish tugged Merryn's hand. 'It hasn't worked. What do we do now?'

'Listen.' Merryn pressed her ear to the post. 'I can hear music. It's starting. I think we've done it.'

The music grew louder. Coloured sparks flew in all directions. They wove themselves into rainbow-coloured threads that twirled and whirled. They swirled round the post, and when they stopped, Kester stood before them. The witch fell back. She clutched her chest and howled in disbelief.

'To the Ringing Stone,' Merryn cried as she leapt onto Kester's back and pulled Hamish up behind her.

Kester galloped for all he was worth, but the witch was close behind. She screamed at her broomstick to go faster. She overtook them and swerved across their path. In her wake came a stream of thick, black smoke. It followed her flight like the vapour trail from an aeroplane.

Kester dashed to one side as he tried to see the way ahead. The witch twisted and turned, circling the bubble until it was enveloped in a cloud so dense that they couldn't see anything. Kester stopped. He gave a frightened whinny and shook his head. Merryn took out the crystal pendulum. It didn't help. Its light bounced back from the wall of smoke. It dazzled her eyes and she had to hide it inside her fleece.

They slipped from Kester's back and discovered why he wouldn't move. The ground all around them was boggy. His hooves were sucked deep into the mud. Their feet began to sink too. They had no idea which way to go. They pleaded with him to keep moving but he refused to take a single step. Remembering her walk through the fog on the day she met Roane, Merryn took the sea-bean box from her pocket and opened it. The tiny shell sent out a beam of light, faint and narrow, but enough to show the way. Kester grew calmer. Tentatively she guided him through the foul-smelling smoke, and when they reached firmer ground, they mounted and were able to go a little faster.

Gradually, the smoke thinned. The moonlight shone through the last wisps and Kester broke into a gallop. The witch was nowhere to be seen, but when they approached the Ringing Stone she was already there. Sitting astride her broomstick, hovering above the stone, she made a hideous silhouette against the circle of the full moon.

'I dare you to draw near,' she shouted. 'Heed my warning. I will not stop until I've destroyed all three of you. I have new and stronger spells to use.'

Merryn felt a tremor run through Kester's body. She leaned forward and spoke into his ear. 'Don't believe her. If she had better spells she'd have used them by now. Make a dash for it. Take her by surprise.'

'Go on,' Hamish yelled. 'You can do it.'

Kester kicked up his heels and cantered towards the witch. The bubble went with them. It threw the witch off balance and it grew to encompass the Ringing Stone. They had arrived, but the witch did not give up the fight. She swerved, pressed her face against the bubble and screamed.

Merryn cringed at the strident sound. Hamish pressed his hands to his ears and cowered down. Kester snorted and pranced. He tossed his mane and his eyes rolled wildly.

It was almost impossible to compete with the shrill of the witch's scream, but she grabbed Kester's head and spoke directly into his ear.

'Close your eyes. Ignore the witch and soon you'll be free.'

Turning angrily to Hamish she pulled his hands away from his ears and shouted an order. 'Pull yourself together. Cover his head. Don't let him see the witch, and keep talking to him.'

Shocked into action, Hamish pulled off his fleece and covered Kester's eyes. Holding it tightly in place, he closed his own eyes and pressed his face into it. Merryn closed her eyes too. She forced her mind go over the things she had to do. When she opened them, Kester and Hamish were standing still.

'That's better,' she cried above the witch's scream. 'Don't move and don't open your eyes until it's over.'

She walked round the Ringing Stone, looking for a starting point, something on the stone that she couldn't possibly forget. One of the cup marks, larger than the others was her choice. Now she was ready. She held the heart-stone in its silken bag in her left hand and she fixed her eyes on the Ringing Stone. She breathed deeply and began to follow the instructions.

With her right hand resting on the stone she walked in a clockwise direction. The first circuit took longer than she'd expected. The ground was uneven, rocky for the most part, but giving way to grass and sand on one side. She shifted her gaze from stone to ground, from ground to stone, carefully avoiding the uneven edge of turf and anxiously looking out for her starting point.

At last, her hand found the hollow of the chosen cup mark. 'One,' she called, and when her voice came back like an echo she knew that the magic was starting.

The witch stopped screaming. 'No,' she shouted, 'no more, no more.'

She flew round the bubble in an anti-clockwise direction. She flew so fast that her passing was nothing but a blur. The sound she made was as loud as a low-flying aircraft, but unlike a plane it didn't fade away into the distance. It went on and on and on.

Merryn wanted to drop to the ground to cover her ears, but she forced herself to keep on walking.

'Two,' she cried.

'Two,' called the echo, 'two..two..two..'

'Stop,' shouted the witch. 'You don't know what you're doing.'

On went Merryn, treading carefully over the bedrock, her right hand moving steadily along the Ringing Stone. The witch stopped circling. She hovered close to the bubble. The pitch of her screams grew higher and higher. Merryn could feel their evil vibrations rippling the surface of the bubble. She tried to go faster, but she tripped and only just managed to keep her hand on the stone. With a gasp of relief she reached the cup mark for the third time.

'Three,' she shouted.

'Three,' came the echo, 'three..three..three..'

'Stop,' shouted the witch as she dived down and smashed into the bubble.

Merryn winced at the impact, but it didn't stop her from completing another circuit. 'Four,' she called.

'Four..four..four..,' repeated the echo.

The witch said nothing. For a moment there was silence. Hamish opened his eyes. Merryn shook her head and he quickly closed them again. She made good progress without the witch's antics distracting her. But before she completed the fifth circuit the witch returned in a spatter of giant raindrops. They drummed on the bubble. They ran down it in waterfalls. The top of the bubble sagged under the weight of water. But it didn't burst.

Still Merryn went on. 'Five,' she cried.

'Five..five..five,' called the echo.

'Hailstones,' shouted the witch, 'bring ice and freezing cold.'

Down came hailstones, big as marbles, big as golf balls. They pelted the skin of the bubble. They slid down the curves and piled up around the outside. In a matter of seconds the bubble was encased in ice. The witch's spells were beginning to work. Although the ice was outside the bubble, it was affecting the inside. Merryn shivered as the temperature fell far below freezing. Her fingers turned blue. The cold crept up her arm. It reached her shoulders and pushed into her chest. She could barely see through the cloud of her own breathing. She struggled on, fighting for breath. Each painful step was slower than the last. Her left hand shook as she clutched the silken bag. When she reached the starting point, she could barely speak through her chattering teeth.

'S..s..six,' she stuttered.

A softer echo bounced back. 'S..s..six,' it called, 's..s..six..s..s..six.'

'Wind,' shrilled the witch, 'come to my aid.'

A great wind came roaring down the sky. It tossed the hailstones away. Its powerful gusts buffeted the bubble, but Merryn didn't pause. Her right hand followed the curve of the stone, and her confidence grew as her feet became familiar with the uneven ground.

'Seven.'

Loud and clear the echo called back.

'Seven..seven..seven..'

'I will not have it,' screamed the witch. 'Sandstorm,' she ordered, 'burst the bubble.'

Instantly, the air was filled with whirling grains. They whipped and lashed the bubble. They rubbed and rasped the surface. They blocked the sight of the witch. They hid the light of the moon. Merryn edged her way through the darkness. Her feet trod carefully over the uneven ground. Her fingers following the curve of the stone searched for the hollow of the cup mark. When she found it her heart leapt, for now there was only one circuit to complete.

'Eight,' she shouted.

'Eight...eight...eight,' came the echo.

The grains of sand swirled away. The bubble filled with the soft glow of moonlight. The witch cursed and flung her broomstick aside.

'Weather,' she commanded, 'do your worst. Deafen them with thunder, strike them with lightning, kill all three of them.'

Chapter 33

At the witch's command, a fork of lightning shot from the sky. It struck the top of the bubble and ran in zigzag lines down the sides. Others followed in quick succession, each one accompanied by a deafening crash of thunder, each one illuminating the bubble in a series of jagged, crackling flashes.

Lightning caught the dry grasses to the seaward side of the Ringing Stone. Tongues of fire spread along the ground and leapt into the air. They licked and lapped at the bubble's skin. Merryn half-closed her eyes against the glare of reflected light. The flames didn't penetrate the bubble but the temperature inside rose higher and higher. She couldn't see where she was going. Drops of sweat ran down her forehead and filled her eyes. With one hand holding the silken bag, and the other touching the Ringing Stone, she could do nothing to wipe them away.

With every crash and flash, Kester stamped his hooves and tossed his head.

'Keep still, Kester,' Hamish begged. 'Hurry up, Merryn. I can't hold him much longer.'

Kester lunged and bumped against Merryn. She managed to steady herself, but her concentration was broken. She couldn't remember how far she'd gone. Where was the cup mark? Had she gone too far? Had she missed it? Almost fainting from the terrible heat, her feet stumbled as grass gave way to rock. Her hand groped its way along the stone until her fingers slipped into the cup mark. Immediately, the flames died away.

Summoning all her strength she shouted, 'Nine.'

'Nine..nine..nine..,' called the echo.

On and on went the echoes until the sky was filled with the sound. The witch wilted. She swayed and dropped onto the sand in a shapeless, shuddering heap. Gradually the echoes died away. When all was quiet, Merryn opened the silken bag and took out the heart-stone.

She had expected something spectacular, a sparkling, shimmering beauty of a jewel, a jewel glowing with magical colours. The thing she held in her hand was nothing but a heart-shaped stone. It was mottled grey in the centre with edges of rusty brown. It couldn't possibly hold enough magic to defeat the witch. Had the Fairy woman cheated her after all? Despair took over until she recalled The Fairy woman's advice. She must believe implicitly in the stone's power. If she doubted, it would be useless.

Pushing away the uncertainty, she placed the heart-stone in her right palm and closed her left hand over it. A slight pulse told her that the heart-stone did indeed hold magic. 'I believe in your power,' she cried. 'Help me to defeat the witch. Help me to save Kester.'

The heart-stone grew warm. The pulse quickened. The stone throbbed like a living breathing thing. Despite its ordinary appearance she knew that it was a stone of tremendous power. Feeling surprisingly confident, she closed her eyes and repeated the words she had learned.

'By the power invested in you please release Kester from the spell that holds him captive.'

The heart-stone throbbed ever more strongly. She counted to nine. She grasped it between the fingers of her right hand and prepared to tap the Ringing Stone. The witch rolled onto her knees and moaned. She crawled towards the bubble and clasped her hands as if in prayer.

'Please, I beg you. Don't tap the stone.' Her voice was thin and wheedling. 'Stop now and I'll do anything you ask.'

Merryn shook her head and tapped the stone. 'One,' she called. A clear ringing filled the air. 'Two.' A second bell joined the first.

'Anything, I'll do anything,' the witch pleaded. 'Stop, I beg you.'

'Three, four, five,' said Merryn. With each tap another bell sounded. Now there were five bells, each one with a different note, yet each one harmonising with the rest.

'Stop,' beseeched the witch. 'I'll release the horse. I promise.'

Merryn grew in confidence as she tapped the stone again and again and again. 'Six, seven, eight,'

Now, the bells rang out in a tune as joyful as any she had ever heard.

The witch grovelled. 'Please, not a ninth bell. You have the power of magic, but you are on the wrong side. Join with me and together we can conquer the world.'

Merryn lifted her hand and tapped the Ringing Stone for the last time. 'Nine,' she shouted. 'We've done it.'

'Nine..nine..nine,' came the echo, 'done it..done it..done it..'

The witch leapt to her feet. Her wheedling tone changed to a roar of anger. 'Curse you. Curse you all.'

A final bell, deep and sonorous joined the others. The sound grew and grew until it was louder than a whole city full of bells. The witch hurled herself at the bubble. She pummelled it. She hammered it with her fists. She butted it with her head. She kicked it and she roared more loudly than she'd ever roared before. But try as she would, she couldn't drown the triumphant ringing of the magical bells.

'Curse you Kester. Curse you interfering brats. Curse you Fairy Folk and curse your heart-stone. May you all be trapped in the fence posts of Tiree for ever.'

Merryn shuddered at the thought. She stood with the heart-stone in her open hand and found herself lost for words. The instructions had ended with the ninth tap. She had no idea what to do next.

The heart-stone took charge. It began to buzz. Its low sound grew until it was louder than a swarm of angry bees. It trembled in Merryn's hand as if it was enraged by the witch's curse. It rose into the air and with a sudden spurt of speed it broke through the skin of the bubble.

'I'll catch you,' shouted the witch as her hand made ready to grab it. 'Your power will be mine and all my curses will come true.'

'No!' Merryn gasped as the heart-stone flew straight towards the witch's open hand.

The witch laughed as her fingers began to close around it. But in the split of a second, the heart-stone darted to one side. It whirled three times round the witch's head. Then it hit her between the eyes. Instantly, the bells stopped ringing. The heart-stone vanished. An expectant silence fell. The witch stood motionless, her mouth open, her face drained of colour.

Hamish clutched Merryn's hand. 'Crumbs,' he said. 'I think…I think she's shrinking.'

Merryn nodded. She swallowed but couldn't speak.

The witch remained in shocked silence. It was not until she was smaller than Merryn that she realised what was happening. She tore her hair and began to shout.

'Break the magic. Make it stop.' She shouted the words over and over, but still she went on shrinking.

When she was smaller than Hamish, she began to howl. She howled and howled and she didn't stop until she was a tiny wee thing, as small as the smallest seashell with a voice no louder than the gentlest breath of breeze. And then she was nothing.

'Crumbs,' Hamish said again. He looked down at the place where the witch had been. He poked the sand with his shoe. He dropped to the ground and began to shake uncontrollably.

'That might have been me,' he whispered.

Merryn's legs gave way. She dropped to her knees and stared. There was no sign of the witch, not a twig of her broomstick, not a shred of her clothes, not a strand of her greasy, grey hair. There was nothing to show that she'd ever existed.

This was what she'd wanted. This is what they'd been fighting for. They'd won. Yet there was something deeply shocking in the way the witch had gone from being alive to being nothing at all.

'It was close,' she whispered. 'If the witch had caught the heart-stone we would have lost. You, and I, and all the Fairy Folk would have been locked inside the fence posts for ever... and Kester...'

She looked round, and her heart leapt when she saw him standing there, alive and free at last. Jumping to her feet, she flung her arms round his neck.

'It's all over,' she said. 'The witch has gone. You're safe. Come on, let's go and tell Aunt Aggie. When she sees you she'll understand why we had to go out at night. Everything will be fine.'

'It won't,' said Hamish. 'He's a magical horse. Aunt Aggie won't be able to see him.'

Merryn sighed. 'I'd forgotten that, but I don't care. We've saved him and that's all that matters. He can take us back to the cottage and we'll just have to put up with whatever Aunt Aggie decides.'

She mounted, pulled Hamish up behind her and turned away from the Ringing Stone. Without the worry of the witch, the ride was so carefree and exhilarating that she didn't notice where they were heading. It was not until she saw the glitter of moonlight on the sea that she realised he was taking them in the wrong direction.

'Stop, Kester,' she ordered. 'We should be going the other way.'

Totally ignoring her words, he left the road and turned onto a narrow track. She tugged his mane as she tried to make him stop, but still he went on.

'Please,' she begged, 'take us to the cottage.'

He galloped even faster. There was nothing she could do to stop him. Over the dunes he went. He rushed onto a long stretch of sand, his hooves thundering as he headed straight for the sea. Suddenly, something she'd read came into her head. Fear clutched her heart. What if he wasn't an ordinary horse at all? What if he had tricked them? What if he was a water horse, a horse that enticed children onto its back and drowned them?

Chapter 34

Merryn tried to make Kester stop, but however hard she tried, it made no difference to his pace. He still galloped straight ahead and the sea was growing closer.

'Hamish,' she screamed. 'We've got to get off.'

'No,' Hamish shouted. 'This is brilliant.' And he clung even tighter to Merryn's waist.

She untangled her fingers from Kester's mane and was about to slide off his back when he veered away from the sea. Weak with relief she gave up trying to stop him. She couldn't understand what was happening. The witch had gone but something else was making him hurry. She didn't know what it was, or why. There was nothing she could do. Along the edge of the waves he went, galloping so fast that he seemed to be flying. He panted and snorted as if he was out of breath, but he didn't slow down. He galloped on towards the rocks at the far end of the bay, and it was not until he almost crashed into them, that he slowed to a trot.

Now she knew where they were. This was where he'd brought her on their first night together. This was where the sporran had been hidden in the sand. He turned into the same tiny cove and passed along the same narrow passageway as before. And once again, he stopped when he reached the high tide line.

'Kester,' she asked, 'why have you brought us here? We've got to get back to the cottage before Aunt Aggie misses us. Please take us back.'

'Yes,' Hamish added. 'We're in enough trouble as it is.'

Kester tossed his head. He whinnied and pawed at the sand. Merryn watched in bewilderment. This time she had no idea what he wanted.

'If you won't take us we'll have to walk,' Hamish complained. 'I don't even know where we are. It'll take hours to find our way and I'm tired and I think you're jolly mean. We rescued you and we got rid of the witch. Now it's your turn to help us.'

Kester paid no heed. He stamped his hooves and gave an urgent, frantic neigh. It was even more desperate than the one Merryn had heard on the very first night.

'I don't think he can take us anywhere,' said Merryn. 'Something's wrong. Get down, Hamish. Quick.'

Hamish slid down onto the sand and Merryn followed. Kester stopped pawing and stamping. A violent tremor rippled through his body. He stood with his head hanging, his body shaking, his coat turning slick with sweat. His breathing grew heavier, harsh rasping in-breaths followed by coughing spluttering out-breaths.

Merryn held the sides of his face and tried to look into his eyes, but he wouldn't open them. Fear flooded through her. She stepped back and chewed on her knuckles. 'He's ill. We need help. Go and get the farmer, he'll know what to do.'

Hamish looked along the length of the beach and then at Merryn. 'I don't know where we are. I don't know which way to go.'

'Just get on the dunes and look for the track.' Her words poured out faster and faster. 'Find the road. Go to the first house you can find. Ask them to phone the farmer. Go on, hurry.'

Hamish started to run, but he'd only gone a few steps when Merryn called him back.

'It's too late,' she shouted. 'Come and help with the crystals.'

Kester's breathing grew ever more laboured. Sweat ran down his face. It dripped from the end of his nose. His legs buckled, his body swayed. He toppled over and lay on his side.

Merryn suspended the crystal pendulum above his head. It gave one flash of brilliant white light before swinging round in a single slow circle. Then it stopped. It changed to cloudy grey as if it was exhausted and no longer held the power of magic. She pushed it and tried to make it swing, but it hung, stiff and straight and wouldn't move at all.

The sporran opened and she thrust the crystals at Hamish. He put the purple one on Kester's side, the yellow one on his head and the pink one near his tail. The figure of eight began to flow round the horse's body, but it didn't make him move.

'Kester's Book,' Merryn gasped. 'Please, tell us what to do. But although the sporran was open, Kester's Book did not appear. She grasped it and tried to pull it out, but the sporran held it fast. 'Please,' she begged. 'Help us.'

The book did not respond and neither did Kester.

'It's no good. It's not working,' Hamish sobbed. 'He's going to die. It's horrible. How can he die after all the trouble we've taken to save him?'

'I don't know,' she sobbed, 'but we've nothing else to try. It's as if his book knows it can't help. I don't understand. Kester,' she pleaded. 'Open your eyes. Look at me. Please.'

For a fraction of a second, his eyes flickered and met hers. They were dark pools of pain. She tried to put her arms round his neck, but although she could see him, she could no longer feel him. She tried to grasp his mane but her fingers passed right through it.

'No,' she sobbed. 'No. You can't disappear now.'

'Get back,' Hamish yelled. He grabbed her arm and tried to pull her away. 'Get back or you might disappear too.'

Merryn refused to move. Hamish let go and fell back weeping. The strands of Kester's mane, his tail and his forelock merged with a swirling mist that rose from the sand. His glossy black coat grew dull. It turned to grey, dark at first, then paler and paler. Merryn tried again to clutch him. There was nothing to hold. He was changing into a ghost of a horse, a phantom that faded and faded until it disappeared entirely.

She stared, white-faced at the place where he'd been. There on the sand lay the necklace of sea beans and hag-stones. There lay the three crystals, yellow, purple and pink. They still wove their figure of eight. They still filled the cove with light. Only what use were they now?

'I can't bear to see them,' she said. 'They're useless. They let us down. Put them away.'

Before Hamish bent to pick them up they slipped inside the sporran.

'What about the necklace,' he asked. 'Look, it's shrinking too. I hope it isn't going to disappear.'

'I don't care if it does,' said Merryn. 'Kester's gone so I don't need it now.' She watched as the spaces between the sea-beans and hag-stones became gradually smaller. Soon it looked exactly as it had looked on the day she first saw it.

'I think you should wear it,' said Hamish. 'There's still magic around. I can feel it. I'm sure I can.'

Merryn shook her head. 'No. It's all over. I don't want it.'

She left it lying where it had fallen. The danger they had been in, the horror of it all suddenly overwhelmed her. She stumbled and leaned against the rock. What had it been for? The witch had gone, but so had Kester. As far as she was concerned, the whole point of the Quest had been for one reason and one reason only. It had all been to set Kester free. All the tasks and challenges had been for nothing. At the last minute, just when she thought they'd won, something had gone horribly wrong. Kester had disappeared, vanished into the moonlit air. She'd failed. She hadn't rescued him at all. Her feet slid from under her, she slumped down on the sand and began to moan.

Chapter 35

Merryn's moans echoed from the nearby rocks. They filled cove with an eerie mournful sound. Hamish grabbed her by the shoulders and shook her.

'Stop it,' he sobbed. 'Stop it. You're scaring me.'

Merryn flung out her arms and pushed him away. She buried her face in her hands. She rocked herself backwards and forwards and she kept on moaning.

'Look, Merryn, look,' Hamish took hold of her hands and tried to pull them away from her face. 'You've got to look. Something's happening. It isn't all over. You've got to believe me.'

'I won't believe anything ever again. I don't believe in magic. I don't believe I have The Gift. I don't believe in witches, or Fairy Folk or Selkies.' Her voice rose in anguish. 'I don't even believe in Kester.'

Tears of disappointment coursed down her cheeks. 'It was all a dream.' She blew her nose and wiped her eyes. 'Only you were right. It wasn't a dream. It was a nightmare. It was the beastliest nightmare that anyone ever had. How could I have been so stupid? How could I have believed that there was a horse trapped inside a fence post?'

'You believed because it was true.'

The voice she heard did not belong to Hamish. She clapped her hands over her ears and shook her head.

'Leave me alone,' she shouted. 'I've had enough magic. I don't want to hear any more. I just want to go back to being an ordinary girl.'

'I know,' said Hamish, 'and I don't blame you. Only it's not as bad as you think. Come on, Merryn. Look up. You've got to.'

'Your brother is concerned for you, as indeed am I. Raise your head, Merryn. Look at me.'

Although she didn't raise her head, she couldn't deny her curiosity. She took her hands away from her ears and she opened her eyes. On the sand in front of her she could see the frayed bottoms of her brother's jeans. She could see his muddy trainers. And next to them, she could see a pair of boots, strange boots such as she'd never seen before. They were of dark blue leather, without laces, without fastenings of any kind. A seam ran down the middle and ended in a short, upturned curl.

She blinked, stared at them again and raised her eyes a little. Now she could see trousers of rich Royal blue. They were narrow-legged and tucked inside the boots. Higher still was a tunic, fashioned of the same fabric. It hung loose, and looked as if it ought to be held in place by a belt, a belt with a sporran! All around its hem, embroidered in gold thread, was the pattern that goes on and on for ever.

'No!' She rubbed her eyes in disbelief. 'I'm dreaming again and I want it to be over. Go away, whoever you are.'

'I promise on my life that you are not dreaming,' said the voice. 'Come Merryn, stand up and look at me.'

Hands reached down, clasped hers and pulled her to her feet. She stood face to face with a boy who looked about the same age as herself. Embarrassed, she tried to pull her hands away, but the boy would not let go.

'I am Kester Witchbane,' he said, 'and I owe my life to you.'

'But,' Merryn struggled to put her jumbled thoughts into words. 'You were a horse. How could you turn into a boy?'

'In my world,' he explained. 'Each and every one of us has a familiar, an animal with which we identify, and whose qualities we share. My familiar is the horse, the horse you knew as Kester. He and I are one. Our lives are intertwined and interchangeable. Sometimes it serves me best to be a boy. At other times I fare better as a horse.'

'Cor! That's cool,' said Hamish. 'But how do you change from one to the other?'

'Normally it is as quick as thought. This last change from horse to boy was tortuous because I had to free myself from the evil of the witch's spell. It required time and a great deal of effort. If you had not thought to use the crystals and the pendulum, I may never have managed it. With your help, the last of the witch's magic has been expelled from my body. Now I am truly free and I should have no further difficulty.'

'So everything's worked out fine for you, but what about us?' Hamish asked indignantly. 'Why didn't you take us back to Aunt Aggie's cottage?'

'I had to change into a boy so that I could speak to you, and I had to return to this cove because this is where I entered your world. When I am fully-fledged I will be able to leave and enter from anywhere. Until then I must retrace my steps exactly.'

An aching emptiness washed over Merryn. She was unable to speak above a whisper. 'You mean you're going away?'

'I am sorry,' he said, 'I have no choice. And now I must ask you to return the things that you have been guarding for me.'

Merryn unbuckled the belt and handed the sporran to him. She lifted the golden chain from her neck and held out the crystal pendulum. To her surprise it was no longer grey and cloudy. As it began to swing, its shimmering colours filled the cove. They shone far across the sea and travelled high into the sky.

'It's beautiful,' she whispered. 'It's the most beautiful thing I've ever seen.' A lump formed in her throat and her eyes filled with tears. 'I don't expect I shall ever see it again.'

'At least you've seen it,' said Hamish. 'I don't understand it. I know it's there because I can see that you're holding something. And I know it can do magic because it mended the bubble after the witch burst it, but I can't see any colours. It's not fair.' He turned to Kester. 'Why can she see it when I can't?'

'Merryn can see magical things because she was born with The Gift,' Kester explained. 'When you picked up the yellow crystal, I was able to lend some of my special powers to you. Now that the Quest is over, I am afraid that you will lose the ability. However, for a few moments, I think you deserve to see the true beauty of my pendulum.'

He reached out his hands and passed them across Hamish's eyes.

Hamish looked up at the sky. He turned round very slowly. His mouth fell open and his eyes grew wide. 'Wow!' he cried. 'It's like the Northern Lights, only it's a million times bigger and a trillion times brighter too.'

Kester waited until Hamish had turned full circle before he took the pendulum from Merryn's hand. He slipped the chain over his head, and as he tucked the pendulum inside his tunic, the colours faded away.

'That was awesome,' Hamish whispered, 'truly, truly awesome.'

'Then hold onto the memory of it,' said Kester, 'for Merryn is right. I do not think you will see its like again.'

He turned to the east. Merryn followed his gaze. As yet there was no sign of light along the horizon.

'I must leave before the sun is up,' he said, 'but I can stay awhile. Your bravery has earned an explanation. So I will tell you something of my story. When I have finished, you will understand that you have done far more than free a horse from the spell of a witch.'

'Before you start,' said Hamish, 'I want to know something. I know you're not a normal human being, but what on earth are you?'

Chapter 36

'I am an apprentice wizard,' said Kester, 'and I do not belong to your earth. I come from a place that is far beyond your imaginings. I ventured into your world before I completed my training, and I have been punished severely for my foolishness. I have wasted time, and I must return to my studies without delay.'

'You mean you bunked off school,' said Hamish. 'Cor! I wish I dare do that.'

Kester shook his head. 'I would not advise you to follow my example. If I had remained at home, I would be a true wizard by now. And I would not have been captured by the witch.'

'But why did she want to capture you?' asked Hamish.

'She knew that I was last in the line of The Grand High Benevolent Wizards. She also knew that much of our strength lies in a bloodline that goes back for many generations. If she had succeeded in breaking the line, Malevolent Witchery would have gained the upper hand.'

'Do you mean if she'd killed you?' Hamish asked.

'That is exactly what I mean,' said Kester. 'It was arrogant of me to think that I could visit your earth and return home without mishap. I wanted to see Tiree, and when I saw the beauty of your ocean I could not resist the chance to swim. I hid my sporran, and knowing that my pendulum would protect me, I entered the water. I saw that the witch was waiting for me. So I changed into a horse in the hope that she would not recognise me. But in so doing, the pendulum must have fallen from my neck. My plan was to change back into a boy, retrieve my sporran and return to my own world. Unfortunately, she realised who I was, and before I reached the cove, she dropped from her broomstick onto my back.'

'Ugh!' Hamish exclaimed. 'That must have been horrible. It was bad enough feeling her through the bubble.'

'I agree,' said Kester. 'It was terrifying, but far worse was the loss of my pendulum. Without its protection my power was much reduced and she was able to trap me inside the fence post. There she left me while she went away to work on stronger spells. She returned again and again. She tried every spell she could think of, but she never managed to end my life. Fortunately, there was a flaw in the spell that held me. Try as she would, she could not hold me captive between midnight and the rising of the sun.'

'I don't understand,' said Merryn. 'If that's true, why didn't you escape? Why didn't you come out of the post every night and try to find your way home?'

'If it were that simple I would have done so long ago,' he said. 'Without my sporran and my pendulum I could not release myself. I needed help. I needed someone with The Gift to hear me. It had to be someone brave enough to seek the things I had lost. That is why I cried for help at midnight.'

'But surely,' said Merryn, 'if your people are wizards they could have rescued you.'

'Yes,' said Hamish. 'Why didn't they?'

'When I lost the pendulum my contact with them was broken. They did not know where to find me.'

He rested his hand on Merryn's shoulder. 'They have you and Hamish to thank for saving me. You have done a far greater service than you can possibly know. The Malevolent Witches set man against man, and country against country. They plan to take control of everything in your fragile world. If you had not released me, my people would eventually have been without a leader, and Malevolent Witchery would have gained in strength.

Merryn felt a tightening in her chest. He was repeating the things that Roane and the Fairy woman had said. She wanted to cry out that it wasn't true, but she had seen the witch, and she knew that many terrible things were happening in the world.

Hamish grasped her arm. 'Crumbs,' he said as he looked at Kester. 'Besides wars and things, do you think they have something to do with floods and earthquakes and volcanoes?'

'It is possible,' Kester answered. 'You saw how one witch was able to call on the weather to help her. If all of them worked together they could do immeasurable harm. Fortunately for us, they are so jealous and suspicious of one another that they never think to share their spells.'

'It sounds as if they're a bit stupid,' said Hamish. 'I mean, even I know that two brains are better than one.'

'Indeed they are,' said Kester, 'and the strength of my people lies in that fact. Each wizard shares his knowledge with all the others. Even so, we need all the assistance we can get. When the Fairy woman whispered in my ear, she pledged the support of the Fairy Folk. That is good to know, but your own people must wake up to what is happening. They too must join the fight.'

He turned to Merryn. 'Let us forget all that for the moment. Our time is short, for now that I have my pendulum, the connection with my father has been re-established. He now knows where I am, and he will expect me to return without delay. I must thank you for braving the sea to return it to me.'

'It wasn't just me. It was Roane who gave it to me,' said Merryn. 'He found it and told me to wear it until I could give it to its true owner.'

Her mind slipped back to the meeting with the Selkie, and farther back to finding the cubbyhole. Suddenly everything fell into place.

'Now I know where it all started,' she said. 'It was the pattern on the wooden box, the one that has no beginning and no end, the one I traced with my finger.' She frowned and tried to remember exactly what had happened when she first went into the cubbyhole. 'Or was it when I drew a horse's head in the dust. I framed it in a circle and wrote my name underneath. I think that's when I first heard the voice calling my name.'

Hamish folded his arms and scowled at her. 'I haven't a clue what you're on about,' he said. 'That's another secret you've been keeping.'

'Just listen,' said Merryn. 'I'll explain later.'

'It was both those things,' said Kester. 'Your drawing was a copy of my personal emblem. Someone, probably my mother, felt the connection and that led them to focus their search on Tiree. The pattern on the box is the symbol of Benevolent Wizardry. When you followed it with your finger, it transmitted a message

225

to my Uncle Tobias. He is The Master of Communications. It told him that you had The Gift, and that you would come to my aid.'

'I don't understand how it could do that,' said Merryn. 'I didn't even know about The Gift until later.'

'You did not need to know. The magic read all that was in your heart.'

A warm glow filled Merryn's chest and a blush rose to her cheeks. 'See,' she said as she pointed to the sporran. 'The pattern is there too. It's on the belt and on the cover of your book. It's even on your tunic. It hasn't got a beginning and it hasn't got an end.' She paused and looked at him. 'I wondered what it meant. Now I think I know. It's about something that keeps going for ever. That's it, isn't it?'

'Exactly so,' he said. 'It means for ever and ever. It promises that our fight against evil will never end.'

'Now I understand,' she said. 'Only that doesn't explain why the box is on Tiree, or how you came to know about it.'

'I know because it was made by my father,' said Kester. 'As to why it is on Tiree, well, there is a story behind that too. When my father was a young man, he came to Tiree. Many were the times he told of the beauty of the white shell sand beaches, the clear seas and the wide skies. That is why I was eager to see the island for myself.'

He touched Merryn's hair and looked deep into her eyes. 'He spoke too of a girl, a girl like you with hair the colour of bracken in autumn and eyes that were flecked with gold.'

Merryn gasped in amazement. The words were familiar. They were the same words that Roane had used. 'It was my great-great-great-great-grandmother, Merryn MacQueen!'

'It was indeed, and I was so caught up in the romantic detail of the story that I failed to heed the rest of it. You see, he too met with evil. Merryn saved his life as you have saved mine. To show his gratitude he gave her the box.'

'Then what happened?' Hamish asked.

'He returned to his own world and married my mother. They have had a good life together and he loves her dearly. Yet we all know that there is a place in his heart that will always belong to Merryn MacQueen.'

Hamish put two fingers in his mouth and pretended to be sick. Merryn, shocked at the rude gesture, dug him in the ribs with her elbow.

'Get off,' he said. 'All that lovey-dovey stuff is too soppy for words.'

'One day,' said Kester with a wry smile, 'you will think differently. You too will know what it is to fall in love.'

'No, I jolly well won't.' Hamish almost exploded at the thought. 'I hate girls, except Merryn of course. She's all right, but that's only because she's my sister.'

Kester laughed, and then his expression grew serious. He looked again at the eastern sky, at the rosy light that was pushing back the darkness.

'I am sorry,' he said, 'but very soon I must say farewell.'

Chapter 37

Kester put one arm round Merryn and the other round Hamish. 'Leaving you will be hard and going home will be difficult. I will have to explain my actions to my father. I hope he will forgive me, for I have only done as he did before me. At least I return far wiser than I was before. The experience has taught me a great deal.'

'Like what?' Hamish asked. 'I can't see how you learned anything when you were stuck inside a fence post.'

'There you are in error,' said Kester. 'It may seem strange to you, but I had eyes and ears and a heart that refused to accept defeat. I learned patience and endurance.'

His face broke into a smile. 'I learned too that all is not lost. As long as mortals like you are prepared to risk their lives to combat evil, there is hope.'

Hamish shivered. 'It really was serious, wasn't it? We could have died, couldn't we?'

'Indeed you could,' said Kester. 'If you had not obeyed my instructions, and if your courage had failed you, my story, and yours would have had a very different ending. But let us not dwell on what might have been. That particular witch has gone forever. I am free, and thankfully, you are none the worse for your experience.'

'Oh, but we are,' said Hamish. 'We're going to be sent...'

'Shh! That's for us to sort out,' said Merryn. 'Kester has problems of his own to face.'

Kester raised his eyebrows and looked questioningly from Merryn to Hamish. 'If by rescuing me you have brought trouble on yourselves I wish to know. There may be something I can do to help.'

'I doubt it,' said Hamish. 'You haven't seen Aunt Aggie when she's in a temper. She's real scary. I'm telling you, we're really for it.'

'I do not understand what 'for it' means,' said Kester. 'Please explain.'

'It means that we're going to be punished. We've been in trouble ever since we got to Tiree. We were told not to go out at night and we kept doing it because we had to help you. We're supposed to be having a holiday. Only we haven't had one because we've spent all our time rescuing you.'

'Hamish, please. Don't go on about it,' said Merryn.

'No. Let him finish,' Kester insisted.

'Well,' said Hamish. 'Last night Aunt Aggie locked the doors so we couldn't get out. We had to climb out of a window. If we're not in our beds when she wakes up she'll send us back to mum and dad. They'll be furious. They'll probably ground us for the rest of the holidays.'

Kester raised his hand to silence Hamish. He turned to Merryn. 'Help me to understand. You need to return to the cottage, but you cannot get in because the doors are locked. Is that correct?'

Merryn nodded.

'But there is an open window?'

'Yes,' she said, 'only it's high up and we can't reach it. We had to jump down. It was the only way we could get out.'

'And you did all this for me?'

'We had to,' said Hamish. 'Remember, you made us promise to go on to the very end.'

'We only had one chance to use the heart-stone,' Merryn added. 'We had to take it.'

'So you see,' said Hamish. 'You're going to be all right and we're...'

'Hamish, that's enough,' said Merryn.

'No. It is not,' said Kester. 'You must tell me all. I am honour bound to help you. He took the yellow crystal from the sporran and tossed it in the air. He caught it deftly on the tip of his first finger and held it in front of Hamish's eyes. It spun round and round like a top, and when it stopped he gave it to Hamish.

'Thanks,' said Hamish, 'but how is it going to help?'

'It will solve your problem. You will both pass through the locked door, and your Aunt Aggie will sleep until you are safely in your beds.'

'No kidding!' Hamish exclaimed. 'Does that mean we can use it all the time?'

'No, Hamish,' said Kester with a wry smile. 'That would be asking too much. It will work once and once only. After that it will lose its magical properties entirely. It will be nothing more than a keepsake.'

Hamish's face fell. 'I thought it was too good to be true,' he said. 'But hang on a minute. Aunt Aggie will still be mad at us. She won't forget what we did yesterday. She'll tell mum and dad and we'll still be for it.'

'The crystal will take care of that too,' said Kester. 'Your Aunt Aggie will forget all your misdemeanours.'

Hamish looked bewildered. 'All our what?' he asked.

'Misdemeanours,' Merryn repeated. 'It means our bad behaviour, all the things we've done to upset her.' She frowned and looked at Kester. 'The only other person who knows is Donald. He might remind her. Do you think you could make him forget too?'

'Consider it done,' said Kester.

'Wow!' Hamish laughed out loud. Then he stopped suddenly. 'You're not going to make me forget, are you? I don't want to forget. I want to tell my friends, although I don't suppose they'll believe me.'

Kester's face grew grave. 'You must never speak of what has happened. If another witch learns of the part you played, she will seek to destroy you. But in any case, you cannot tell, for we have an agreement. You asked me to stop your words if you thought to speak of the magic. That will apply for ever, and I am sorry to disappoint you, but the memory will fade. It will seem like a half-forgotten dream. But should another challenge come, you will remember everything. The experience gained in this Quest will help you to face another one.'

The happy smile vanished from Hamish's face. 'But I don't want another one. I don't want to fight another witch. I just want to find out about rock pools and birds and things that aren't trying to kill me.'

'I am not ready for another fight either,' said Kester, 'but future battles lie beyond our control. If the call comes I will have to answer. Because she possesses The Gift, Merryn will have to answer too. You have proved your bravery and I am sure that when the time comes, you will help her.'

Turning to Merryn, Kester placed the pink crystal in her palm and folded his hands over hers. 'Keep it with you always. You have The Gift so it will retain its magic. It will also maintain its connection to me. Should you have need of me, clasp it in your hand and speak my name. If I cannot come, I will send someone else to your aid. Benevolent Wizards cannot solve everything, but if right is on your side, we will do everything in our power to help you.'

He picked up the necklace of sea-beans and hag-stones and slipped it over Merryn's head. 'This belonged to the first Merryn MacQueen. Wear it always, for I believe you will need its protection.'

Merryn gulped. 'Not more magic, not now, not yet, please. Anyway, I can't keep it. It belongs in the box. It belongs on Tiree.'

He shook his head. 'No, it belongs to you now, for you have truly earned it. The box is also yours. When you leave the island, you must take it with you. It has your name upon it, and I know that my father would want you to have it.'

Merryn followed his glance as he looked once more towards the east. Any second now, the sun would rise. With one last squeeze of her hand he stepped away. He held up the purple crystal and touched the rock face.

Merryn choked on a sob. There were so many things she wanted to ask, so many things she wanted to say.

'Wait...'

She took a step towards him, reached out her hand and called his name. 'Kester, please wait.'

But he passed through the rock without a backward glance, and she was powerless to follow.

THE HAGSTONE CHRONICLES
CRY AT MIDNIGHT

How the book came to be written.

Out to the west of Scotland lie the remote islands of the Inner and Outer Hebrides. One of the most beautiful is the Isle of Tiree. While on holiday there I found an old fence post in the shape of a horse's head – and out of that my book was born.

I stayed in a cottage just like Aunt Aggie's and as I walked around the island, real places found their way into the story. I read about Fang an t-Sithean in an old book, but no-one I asked knew its name or its location. A bit of detective work with books and maps led me to the small mound with its rocky summit and tumbled wall. I placed my ear against the Ringing Stone and tapped it with a pebble. The bell-like sound it made was truly magical. I saw moon daisies growing on The Reef and I had a picnic in the tiny cove at the south end of Traigh nan Gilean. I found a tiny purple-tinged shell, a stone in the shape of a heart, a hag-stone and a sea-bean.

I didn't find the suterain. No-one could tell me where it was. So this underground dwelling from the days when lives were at risk from invaders became an ideal hiding place for the witch. Because of the low, windswept nature of the island, Tiree has only a few very stunted trees. However, in 1959, Ake-ake trees, natives of New

Zealand, were introduced. They form hedges around many gardens and some of them have grown into mature trees.

When I returned to my home on the Isle of Islay. I hung a photograph of the fencepost on the wall of my writing cabin. After a heavy storm, rain seeped in, the curtain was soaked and the colours ran into the picture, adding shades of blue, pink and purple. This gave me the idea for the coloured threads that appeared when the horse emerged from the post.

Throughout my story there are patterns that never end and the final magical discovery came when I learned that the Maori word Ake-ake means for ever and ever.

To see pictures of the places in the story, to ask questions (which I will answer), or to make comments about the book, please visit my website: mavisgulliver.co.uk

CLICKFINGER by Mavis Gulliver

Available July 2015

Merryn and Hamish MacQueen think that a cottage on the tiny island of Kerrera will be the perfect place to spend their summer holidays. There are wild goats and otters to watch; and there are beaches, cliffs, caves and the ruins of an ancient castle to explore.

To Hamish, their adventure on Tiree is as vague as a half-forgotten dream. To Merryn it is as clear as if it happened yesterday. She could never forget the horse that called at midnight or the challenges she had to face. Most of all she remembers Kester, the young wizard. Her dearest wish is to see him again, but the chances of that ever happening are very remote indeed.

She treasures the crystal that he gave her. The necklace of sea-beans and hag-stones still hangs round her neck, but since the death of the Tiree witch it has been still and silent. On their very first day on Kerrera everything changes. The necklace begins to throb – a sure sign that there is magic in the island air.

So begins another adventure, one that is even more perilous than the last. There are many children involved. All of them are in danger and only Merryn has the power to save them.